"Don't fraternize with the enemy this close to game time!"
—Marvin told the Bears. But:

Rudi Stein was learning a new submarine pitch—Oriental style.

Engelberg was telling his troubles to a Japanese shrink.

Tanner, Toby, Ahmad, and Feldman were watching the great Sadaharu Oh as guests of the Tokyo team.

Kelly and his new Japanese girlfriend were off on a picnic.

Even Marvin himself was doing something mysterious with a geisha. (He didn't see Ahmad's little brother tagging along . . .)

And on the morning of the big game both teams disappeared! Yomiuri Stadium was packed. Marvin and the Japanese coach were frantic. The ABC program director was going berserk . . .

WHERE WERE THE BAD NEWS BEARS?

PARAMOUNT PICTURES PRESENTS

THE BAD NEWS BEARS GO TO JAPAN

Starring
TONY CURTIS

Written by
BILL LANCASTER

Produced by
MICHAEL RITCHIE

Directed by
JOHN BERRY

A Paramount Picture

THE
BAD NEWS BEARS
GO TO JAPAN

RICHARD WOODLEY

Based on the screenplay by
BILL LANCASTER

A DELL BOOK

ONE

The long white banner draped over the center-field fence riffled in the breeze. The strong sun glinted off the red lettering. The list was professionally painted:

TOKYO GIANTS—1967 WORLD CHAMPIONS.
WAKAYAMA RED SOX—
1968 WORLD CHAMPIONS.
TAI PEI TIGERS—1969 WORLD CHAMPIONS.
T'AI'NAN BRAVES—1971 WORLD CHAMPIONS.
TAI PEI INDIANS—1972 WORLD CHAMPIONS.
T'AI'NAN ORIOLES—1973 WORLD CHAMPIONS.
T'AI'NAN ORIOLES—1974 WORLD CHAMPIONS.
CHOFU TIGERS—1976 WORLD CHAMPIONS.

That the nicknames of the teams, and all the lettering on the banner, were in English—the only representation of that language among the many signs and posters around the field—was testimony to the game's genesis. But the places and dates listed testified to more recent history, during which small-fry baseball was lately being played best half a world away from the game's place of origin.

As on this day. No kids anywhere in the world were playing better ball than was being played here on this field. The mannerisms and gestures and styles and equipment were the clear, direct heritage of the Great American Game. The pitcher scratched a cleated foot around the pitcher's mound and fingered the rosin bag as he stared in at the catcher. The catcher pounded his fist into his mitt, then extended two fingers down to call for a curve ball. The batter spat off to the side as he dug in, his hands working around the grip of the bat. Runners took cautious leads off second and third. The crowd, ready to cheer or moan in a few seconds, was hushed, holding its breath.

The pitcher wound up, kicked his left leg high, and delivered. The batter stepped into the pitch and swung. The ball dipped under his bat, thudding into the catcher's mitt.

The umpire snapped his right arm up. His shout of the third strike was drowned out by the eruption of cheers from the hometown crowd.

Teammates of the beaming twelve-year-old pitcher raced onto the field and enveloped him, hopping and yelling congratulations, deep into the ecstasy of winning.

Members of the losing team clustered silently in and around their dugout, tears streaming down their faces. They glanced occasionally out at the happy winners, shaking their heads sadly, their expectations and energy of minutes before suddenly and totally drained.

It was the classic scene of victors and vanquished.

The scoreboard registered the final score: Team Japan 1, Team Taiwan 0.

Atop the flagpole to one side of the scoreboard, the rising-sun flag flapped gloriously, as if it too celebrated the triumph of the country's young ballplayers.

Far away, another rising-sun flag of Japan flapped in the wind. But this flag, tattered from bullet holes and begrimed with soot and smoke, whipped ingloriously above a destroyed bunker in the heat of battle.

This flag, which quickly fell, was being seen in the United States, on a TV screen. The movie was the old World War II film, *Back to Bataan*. John Wayne, a head taller than his own troops and twice as big as any of his foes, charged through the thick jungle fanning a machine gun ahead of him. All around, the one-sided fire fight raged, American soldiers blasting into the bush and blowing sinister-looking Japanese from sniper posts in palm trees.

John Wayne had been, for a generation, or maybe two, the symbol of patriotic might through one war after another, from those with American Indians to those with Orientals. For his size and looks and confident sense of right and justice, he endured as the ultimate hero, even to those too young to have experienced, or even to appreciate, war.

And on this sunny Saturday morning in a small living room of a small San Fernando Valley home in California, John Wayne was again the ultimate hero for a small boy named Tanner Boyle.

Tanner, a sturdy but pint-sized twelve-year-old, sprawled on his stomach seven inches from the tube. The set he was watching was black-and-white, which is the way Tanner saw things anyway—almost everything. A couple of new facial bruises glowed blue in the light of the screen, and a fresh scab glistened red on his cheekbone—all marks from a brief altercation of the day before when somebody had said something that Tanner didn't even remember exactly, but which had been harsh enough to challenge Tanner's honor.

Tanner did not—anymore than John Wayne—consider himself a violent person. But where honor and justice were concerned, Tanner was not one for verbal debate. He was not so good with words. He was not much better with his fists, but, win or lose, those fists gave him self-respect. As he stared raptly, seldom even blinking, at the TV, he wished he had the size and strength of John Wayne, and a suitable enemy against which to assert himself. It was not, he felt, an idle wish, for when you are twelve all things are possible, even growth.

Tanner, though by far the most engrossed in the movie, was not alone in the room. Several other boys, mostly of about his age, were scattered about. Beside him on the rug, similarly prone, was the youngest, Rasula Abdul Rahim, who was eight, and whose major wish at the moment was that his Afro were as bushy as that of his twelve-year-old brother, Ahmad, who sat behind him with his arms clasped around his knees. The brothers, nearly inseparable because of Ahmad's impatient protectiveness, were members of one of the few black families in the neighborhood, though not even Tanner perceived them any longer as black, because the brothers were his teammates.

E.R.W. Tillyard III, thin and studious, lounged in a frayed armchair and peered through his thick glasses into a book called *The Encyclopedia of Curling*. Occasionally he shook his head at a disputable bit of logic, or nodded at an incontrovertible fact, as he read about the quaint, shuffleboard-like sport in which people slide big, round "stones" down an ice rink toward teammates who sweep the ice with brooms to retard the stones' progress. Tillyard, though he played ball sometimes, was mostly the team's statistician.

Toby Whitewood, Rudi Stein, and Ahmad conversed about girls—to Tanner, an irreverent distraction from the movie.

8

"Knock it off," Tanner hissed from time to time as their whispers got on his nerves.

Kelly Leak, larger, stronger, and a year or two older than the others, reclined on the sofa and stared at the ceiling. A set of earphones half-covered his ears, and from them was emitted the loud volume of a Led Zeppelin tape. He was smoking a cigarette and sipping from a can of root beer onto which he had stuck a label from a bottle of Budweiser. His attention was divided into three parts: the music, the nearby talk about girls, and the closeby preachments of Jimmy Feldman.

Feldman, not quite as thin and studious as Tillyard, had nonetheless a similar intense and serious look. Even the joyful smile now on his face seemed to carry somber concern. He wore a T-shirt on which was stenciled, "Praise Him!"

On his knees beside the sofa, Feldman leaned close to Kelly to continue his message. ". . . Kelly, once you allow Jesus into your heart, your whole being begins to glow with His love."

Kelly closed his eyes. "Will you bag it, Feldman," he growled.

"I know at first it's hard to accept His love, but—"

Kelly snapped his head around. "What'd you say about her, Whitewood?"

"I said Gail Williamson is ready," Toby said, reading from a stack of index cards in his lap.

"I agree," Rudi said. "That's how she looks to me."

"You guys don't know nothing," Kelly snorted, lying back down and closing his eyes. "You want to know who's ready, you don't need those cards. You just ask me."

". . . His love, you see, conquers all. . . ."

"Knock it off!" Tanner slammed his fist against the floor, his eyes never leaving the movie.

Ahmad and Rudi leaned closer toward Toby, and hushed their voices as he thumbed through more cards.

A clink of dishes came from the kitchen.

"Engelberg!" Tanner hollered. "Get away from my icebox!"

"I ain't nowhere near your icebox!" came the hollered reply.

Engelberg was, in fact, on the opposite side of the kitchen from the refrigerator, rummaging through the cupboards. "You call that thing an icebox? It's like a desert in there! Fellow would starve looking for food in that wasteland!"

Engelberg was, as usual, starving. That fact was not apparent from the way he looked. He was round and huge. Everything on his body bulged, even his fingers. He was the catcher on their baseball team, not because he was so good with his mitt or had so strong a throwing arm, but because few pitches or runners got by his great girth.

Their boys' league team, the "Bad News Bears," had people playing certain positions not because they were skilled at those posts but because by and large they couldn't play anyplace else. Engelberg could neither run nor throw with authority, but when he squatted at the plate, he was an immovable colossus. He was at his best when the bases were loaded against them—as they often were. For a runner to score, he had first to get past Engelberg. With or without the ball at home plate, he was a formidable wall.

"Hate improvising with the cupboards," Engelberg muttered to himself, pushing his hand in among the jars and cans. "No protein. No perishables. No sweet stuff for quick energy. Dumbest kitchen I ever saw."

Then his face brightened. "Raisins!" He pulled out

10

the box and stuck his hand into it. "Not *Hersheys*, but not bad . . ."

"Engelberg!" Tanner barked. "What're you into?"

"Health!" he answered, wolfing down a handful.

Ahmad, who sometimes played right field, unless the team they were playing tended to hit balls out there, wrinkled up his brow in thought. "What about Lucy Mendoza?"

"Developing fast," Toby said, pulling out her card. "You looked at her lately?"

"All you guys can do is *look*," Kelly grumbled.

"Stop, look, and listen," Feldman crooned, leaning toward Kelly. "That's a good motto for being in position to accept His teachings. . . ."

"Feldman, *you* stop. *I'm* listening. I'm trying to hear this riff. Nobody riffs like Led Zepp."

Miguel Aguilar, small, with dark, soulful eyes, turned his head toward each of the speakers in turn, saying nothing. He spoke little English. Upon moving into the area from Mexico he had joined the team, in fact, to try to learn the language.

Tanner grimaced and turned away from the screen. "Can't watch this next part."

"Why not?" Rasula's eyes widened expectantly at the TV.

"This is where William Bendix gets it. Makes me sick every time."

"William who?"

Tanner's heroes were old ones, largely from old war movies like this one, where issues were clear and simple. Before William Bendix could get it, he switched channels.

The new program was "Kids in the News." The narrator was in mid-sentence.

". . . although the jubilation the young Japanese team experienced after beating the tough Taiwan team was rather short-lived. Later they were informed that their invitation to a United States team was turned down by the National Young Men's Baseball Association here in America . . ."

Toby Whitewood (often the Bears' first-baseman, known for hugging the bag as if it were a security blanket—which, in a way, it was, such was his fear at any ball hit toward him) jumped from the rug and turned up the sound. "Hey, this is about the Japanese champs!"

". . . So our correspondent in Japan asked the Japanese boys and their coach what they thought of the American refusal."

The scene switched to a TV studio in Japan. Coach Shimizu, a stocky, unsmiling man of about forty-five, was being interviewed. He spoke Japanese. A translator spoke into the mike.

"We were surprised and a bit hurt," Shimizu said through the translator, neither man showing any emotion. "It was simply a gesture of international friendship and sportsmanship on our part. We thought it would be a . . ." The translator looked at Shimizu, who repeated some words. ". . . splendid notion to bring together boys from such different parts of the world to play a game which we now have in common among us."

The scene shifted again to one of the small players, still in uniform. The same translator performed his work. "One of the reasons the U.S. gave for not coming," the boy said, "was because they say we're too competitive. That's plain dumb. Baseball is baseball."

The camera panned to another boy, who looked

indignant. "I think they're just plain chicken," came the translation.

"What'd that little foreign crud say?" Tanner snarled, jumping up.

"He's right," Kelly said.

The Bears gathered around the TV as the interviews continued. But they no longer listened.

Tillyard raised an index finger to straighten his glasses. "It is true that the Oriental teams have beaten the United States entries six out of the last eight times we've played them."

"'Cause why?" Tanner said, looking at him doubtingly.

"'Cause they're good," Kelly said. Then he put his earphones back on and closed his eyes.

Tanner was furious. He stomped back and forth in front of the TV. "Well, I just can't believe we're chicken. I mean, we invented the game, didn't we?"

"We also invented the automobile," Tillyard said, tipping his nose into the air. "But the best race drivers are French, Italian, and British."

"Hog pies," Tanner growled. "None of that's true. We drive the best and we play ball the best. Foreigners are always trying to horn in."

"Not horn in," Tillyard asserted, "just *get* in. In many cases they improve upon what we have invented. Especially the Japanese. And the Japanese especially in baseball. Their professional teams are not far behind ours now. And apparently their kids teams are already better than ours."

"No way! They ain't played *us* yet!"

"Who's us?" Rasula asked.

"The Bears, that's who!"

"Of course not, Tanner," Tillyard said. "They

haven't played us because we haven't even won our own championship right here in this league. To say nothing of the state championship. To say even less of the national championship."

"Well, I say they ain't got nothin' to claim until they've played us."

Tanner Boyle was the Bears' shortstop. At first he had taken that position because he was short, just as the name seemed to call for. But it turned out to be the best position for him after all because, although he didn't catch everything hit toward him, he stopped most balls, whether that meant diving, falling, sliding, or just letting them hit him in the chest. He was fearless and quick. And when a runner tried to slide into second, he had to deal with Tanner's arms and head and feet and anything else Tanner could use to protect the base.

"And since they're claiming something or other," Tanner went on, "I think it's time to do something about it."

"Just what you got in mind, Tanner?" Kelly said, sitting up and narrowing his eyes.

"We're gonna play them pip-squeaks," Tanner said, smiling cruelly. "That's what!"

There was a silence.

"How?" Ahmad asked.

"Unh, well, okay, gather round, Bears." Tanner nodded grimly. "We're gonna brainstorm. And nobody leaves my house until we come up with something."

It was an ordinary Saturday night at the offices of United Press International in Los Angeles. Which meant that the banks of teletype machines clacked and chattered and dinged their bells incessantly with streams of news from the area and around the world.

The two news editors on duty, both sporting unshaven faces and loosened ties, busily scratched in penciled changes on the copy. Occasionally one or the other of them got up from his swivel seat to scan the outpourings of the machines, or to sit down in front of the sending machine to type out a story from their own area, or to send a question about details of a story they had received over the wires.

They sipped coffee nervously, answered the phones that kept ringing. Tucking the receivers in between their chins and shoulders, they scribbled down information called in from reporters all over California.

An ordinary Saturday night at the UPI offices had an air of intense and sometimes frantic professional bustle. The editors said little to each other, transmitting opinions and decisions by arcane grunts, shrugs, and mutterings. The news of all the world swirled about them, clacked out by the machines, while they, otherwise in isolation, made quick assessments of the relative worthiness of all the stories, and arrived at snap judgments far more often right than wrong. Hundreds of newspapers that subscribed to the UPI service depended upon their judgments, and deadlines could not be missed.

Into this busy din strode E.R.W. Tillyard III, Tanner Boyle, Kelly Leak, and Michael Engelberg. They stood at the counter watching impatiently until one of the editors noticed them.

"Yeah?" He didn't rise from his seat.

"We have a story for you," Tillyard said, holding up a sheet of lined paper.

"School pages closed two hours ago, kid," the editor said, looking back at the copy he was editing. "You can leave it there if you want. Name and phone number on it."

"It's not a school story," Tillyard said firmly. "It's international. Real news."

"Leave it."

"I think you'll want to send it right out."

He glanced over at the other editor and shook his head. "Okay, okay." He stretched and stood up and walked quickly over. "Gimme your international story."

Tillyard handed it to him. "I don't think you'll have to reword any of it. It's clear and right to the point."

"Hmm." He scanned it briefly. "You boys going to Japan? Sounds nice." He handed it back. "Just leave your release here with your phone number and we'll get back to you." He turned away.

"Sir, I don't think you understand, sir. This is for immediate release."

"Yeah," the editor said, sitting back down at his desk. "Leave it. Leave it immediately."

"But sir—"

"Listen, kid"—he had already resumed working on the copy—"*everything* is for immediate release. The whole world is clamoring for immediate release. We're backed up to here with stories to go out on that sending machine over there. And nothing goes out on that machine"—he waggled his pencil at it—"unless we want it to. And even if we want it to, not until we check sources and verify the story. So just leave the thing here. And *you* leave here, please. We're very busy."

Kelly elbowed past Tillyard. "Look, mister, this is a matter of international importance."

"*You* look, kid," chimed in the other editor, slapping down his pencil and swiveling toward the counter, "you wouldn't know international importance if it bit you in the nose. We simply do not have time to debate the merits of your story right now."

"Well, *make* time. This is news!"

Both editors leaned back and closed their eyes and sighed. During that instant Tillyard slipped past the counter and edged around behind them, toward the sending machine.

Finally the first editor looked over at Kelly and rubbed a hand across his forehead. "Guys," he said in a softened tone, "it's Saturday night, hunh? It's one of our busiest times, understand? It all pours in on Saturday night—murders, robberies, guys with hostages, alarms, false alarms, attempted this and attempted that—everything under the sun. Right now we got a three-alarm fire on Adams. We got some kind of melee in Reseda. All that's local. Then we got a quake in Turkey. We got a troop movement in Syria. We got a suspected kidnapping in France. We got a tin-miners' strike in Bolivia. We got tourists missing in Acapulco. We got the Pope in Tibet, with Lowell Thomas. We got drugs and guns and pomp and circumstance all over the globe. And not only that, the sports scores are gonna come in like an avalanche in about five minutes."

He glowered at Kelly. "So give us a break and get the heck out of here!"

Engelberg elbowed past Kelly. "Well, you guys sure aren't no, unh, Wood, unh, Stern . . ." He huddled quickly with Kelly. Then he puffed up his chest. "You guys sure aren't no Woodward and Bernstein, I'll tell you that!"

The editors sighed and proceeded to ignore them, returning to their work. Suddenly they stopped. "Hey!"

They had spotted Tillyard, who was seated at the

machine, painstakingly typing the story from his sheet of paper.

"Hey! What the devil's going on!" The editor jumped up and raced over.

But by then Tillyard had finished. He leaned back and folded his arms smugly. "I put my name and phone number on it too."

"Oh my blessed begonia!" The editor slapped his forehead. "The kid sent out the blamed story! How we gonna explain this?"

"You got a scoop," Tillyard said, grandly walking out, followed by his smiling friends. "You should be proud."

The Bears strode proudly through the door, accompanied by the moans of the two editors.

It was a relatively dull night at the *Chicago Tribune*. A rewrite man from the national desk leaned over the UPI machine to check the latest contributions. His eye fell on a story the first line of which read: "The famous Boys' League Baseball Team, the Bad News Bears, from California, hereby announces its plans to raise funds to travel to Japan to meet the Far Eastern Champions, who claim to be the World Champs."

The rewrite man knew nothing of the "famous Bears," and cared less about baseball, especially as played by, as he would say, "brats." But something in the wording of the sentence caught his attention. He ripped the story off the machine and took it back to his desk.

"Worst lead sentence I've ever seen," he muttered to an associate. "But there's something appealing about it, like for once it's a story that reads like it was written by a human being instead of a darned machine."

And with that, he marked it up with editing symbols, slapped on a quick headline, and sent it through for the early Sunday edition.

A similar scene took place in the studios of WHC-TV in Hartford, Connecticut. Except that this news editor assumed he had heard quite a bit before about the famous Bears, or should have. He edited it and sent it into the newsroom for a blurb at eleven o'clock.

In several other places across the country the story was picked up and used, most often as a one-paragraph "bright."

But the most important place where the story was spotted was in Tokyo, Japan, where one of the large dailies not only decided to use it, but further determined that it was a major newsbreak. A cable was quickly dispatched to Coach Shimizu of the Far Eastern Champions.

On a small diamond in Kofuku, Coach Shimizu was putting his team through some demanding drills. He lined up his infielders in front of the backstop. Then, standing at home plate some fifteen feet from them, he knocked ground balls at them. The coach was well aware that at that distance most of the balls were impossible to field.

But the drill was not cruel; it was his manner to set the most difficult standards, beyond the reach of any boy to master but within the reach of all to achieve some measure of success. That is, not all the balls were impossible. The boys were dexterous and fearless. With each passing minute, more balls were caught by more-confident hands.

From behind the backstop a small boy came running toward the coach, waving a piece of paper in his hand. He approached Shimizu, bowed, and handed him the cable from the newspaper.

Shimizu read it quickly, raising his eyebrows with

interest. He called the team together, bringing in his other fielders and pitchers from the outfield to join the infielders around him.

"The Americans," he said in lilting Japanese, "have finally seen fit to send a team to play us."

The boys looked at each other, smiles breaking out on their faces. But they controlled their excitement and surprise.

"I understand that it is a volunteer squad of sorts," Shimizu went on, raising his eyes from the cable to look at the team. His looks and words were, as usual, what Americans call "understated." That means that he did not exaggerate. "I am pleased at this news, of course. I expect you boys to be prepared for them, for the game—all of you."

All the boys nodded.

"So. Now is the time for us to end our practice, and for you to return to your studies. The American boys, by the way, do not have school in the summertime. That might seem to give them a small advantage as far as preparing for this game is concerned. But not really. For disciplined use of time in both work and play is the best preparation. It is like our country, where we have so many people and so little room. We make use of every space. Our practices will be more fruitful for the fact that time for them is not precious. Now then"—he carefully folded the cable and put it in his pocket—"I shall inquire for more details of the Americans' visit, and will inform you of all I know at practice tomorrow."

They nodded happily.

The coach raised an index finger into the air, and the boys stiffened expectantly. "It is good and proper for you to anticipate this game with the American boys. But do not forget: Anticipation is valuable only together with activity. Do not daydream idly. Use each hour as you wait for the Americans. Study hard. Practice hard. In that way, what you anticipate cannot fail to be worthy of your expectations."

They all nodded briskly and watched their coach walk away.

Once he was out of view, they relaxed. They broke into cheers and pounded each other on the back. They waved small fists in the air. One reached into his shirt pocket and took out a hidden cigarette and lit it, blowing a circle of smoke into the air and annoying the others with his breach of rules. They said confident things to each other about the skills of their team and how they would demolish the Americans. They said things about how they could hardly wait for the game, that they wished it were tomorrow.

Then some doubts crept into their banter—concern about how good the American team really might be, and about how maybe they had themselves been a bit lucky to win a couple of close games on the way to the championship. They were anticipating, that is to say, to beat the band.

In short, in the absence of their coach, they were behaving and talking more than just a bit like their American counterparts.

TWO

Monday morning, as usual, dawned hard for Marvin Lazar. The early sun beat into the window of his small apartment in West Hollywood, heating the copy of *Daily Variety* that lay across his face.

The night before, Marvin had, as was common for him, fallen asleep on the sofa fully dressed, TV on, empty whiskey glass stinking on the end table near his head.

Now the murmurings of the morning talk show penetrated his dim, hungover consciousness, and he raised his head, the show-biz newspaper sliding down his chest and onto the floor.

He sat up, rubbed his face, and blinked his eyes at the tube. "Good morning, Regis, you crock," he said at the screen, where Regis Philbin was conducting his talk show with a row of minor-sized guests.

Philbin was facing the row of boys, who sat fidgeting in their chairs. "Now, as I understand it, you boys are going against the wishes of your national organization, the National Young Men's Baseball Association, to pursue your unusual effort to get to Japan. Why?"

"Well—" E.R.W. Tillyard III began.

"It's mainly the guidance of the Holy Spirit," Jimmy Feldman piped up. "And the Lamb of God."

"Pardon?" Philbin glanced into the camera with widened eyes.

"We feel strongly," Tillyard put in hurriedly, "that an American team should represent our country in Japan. It seems only fitting, since they extended the, unh, challenge, that—"

"We ain't no cowards!" Tanner Boyle barked. "And we ain't running away from no—"

His last words were bleeped out.

"I see . . ."

"Philbin, you turkey," Marvin mumbled, wearily reaching for the telephone. He dialed, fumbling a few times with his shaking fingers before getting it right.

"Answering service," came a woman's cheery voice.

"Marge? Morning, dear. It's Marvin. You sound sweet and lovely, as always. I continue to imagine you as being beautiful, and shall until we meet one day— and perhaps even after, hmm? You have a message or two for me?"

"A bunch, love. Where you been, Marvin? I tried until late."

"Holding a nervous client's hand until five in the morning. That's where."

"A client? Things are looking up. Somebody famous?"

"No sarcasm, now. No, not anybody famous. A painter. Ten percent of this joker's earnings wouldn't pay my bill for your service."

Through this Marvin kept an eye on the TV, where Tillyard was holding forth.

". . . Also, we feel that if an American team didn't go, it could severely strain relations between otherwise friendly nations. We felt an obligation to—"

"Aw, bull!" Tanner put in. "We just want to kick the . . ."

Bleep, bleep.

"Got a pencil, Marvin?" Marge asked.

"No, but I have a good memory. Shoot."

"Dave Fisher is canceling lunch. Something about being too busy with a new script that may interest Dustin Hoffman. John Pekkanen regrets to say he can't see you for drinks. Something about being on the wagon and not leaving his room. Don Jackson won't be able to meet you for dinner. Something about a hurry-up job covering jai alai for *Sports Illustrated*. Suggests maybe sometime next week."

"Jackson," Marvin grunted as he tried to free his large, golden, chainlike necklace, which had become tangled with the phone cord. "Started out in the mail room at MGM with that turkey."

He looked at the TV.

Tillyard went on. ". . . Well, we plan to pay for the trip mainly by saving and borrowing." He smiled into the camera. "But we are in no way above accepting donations, which would be, I believe, tax deductible. So we will definitely welcome donations."

"You and me both, kid," Marvin said to the screen.

"What?"

"Nothing, Marge. Just mumbling to myself about the state of the arts."

". . . So if you want to," Tillyard continued, giving the camera a beseeching look, "you viewers can send money to: Bears, P.O. Box 1941—"

"We got the 1941 from Pearl Harbor," Tanner interjected. "You know, when the . . ." (Bleep) ". . . bombed us in a sneak attack."

". . . Van Nuys, California."

"Speaking of the state of the arts, Marvin," Marge said, "your ex-wife called from Acapulco to say that the weather is great and she and Pedro are having a wonderful time."

Marvin grunted, watching Tanner on TV.

Tanner had stood up and was unbuttoning his windbreaker. He faced the camera. "Now I want to talk about the *real* reason we're going." He jutted out his jaw. "And it's got to do with this wonderful country of ours, as opposed to this other country."

The legend on his now exposed T-shirt read: "Sony's Baloney and Hondas Hurt."

Tanner strode toward the camera, sticking his face close to the lens so that it appeared distorted on Marvin's screen. "If you'll remember, viewers, this country's called America. And that one is called Japan. That make it *clear* for you?"

Marge was completing her message over the phone. "She also said you should get into some reading about the differences between the sexes. Said she thinks it would help you out."

Marvin grunted again, this time more forcefully.

The camera shifted its angle from Tanner to host Regis Philbin. "Hey," Tanner said angrily. "What are you doing putting the camera on *him?*"

Philbin smiled. "Well now, young man—"

"I'm talking here. Put it on me. Camera's on him all the time. Every stinking morning. People got to be sick of—"

Suddenly the sound was cut off. Tanner's mouth formed oaths.

"And she wanted to remind you," Marge said over the phone, "about the alimony checks for March, April, and May."

Marvin winced and sighed. "Marvelous. All of it's marvelous. Anything else, Marge? Any other nuggets of information?"

"Well, you owe our answering service eighty-two dollars and fifty cents."

"Thank you, Marge."

He hung up and rubbed his face, staring absently at the TV.

Tanner was now being forcibly restrained, held back from Philbin at whom he futilely waved his fists.

"Dave Fisher cancels lunch," Marvin mused bitterly. "Practically gave him the idea for *Airport '81*. So now he thinks he can get Hoffman to read his junky script. Ungrateful turkey."

He stumbled his way toward the bathroom. "And that Pekkanen. On the wagon . . . again. Always goes on the wagon. Right after he drinks himself into a stupor. And right before he drinks himself into another one. Only time he can act is when he stays in his room by himself. Won't have drinks with me because I won't pick up his tab. Cheap, ungrateful turkey."

He fumbled for his can of shaving lather, dropped it, stooped painfully to pick it up.

"And that Jackson. Came on my client list claiming to write for TV. Now he covers jai alai for *Sports Illustrated*. Works a month and gets paid for a week. Deceitful, cheap, ungrateful turkey."

He lathered his face and stared at himself in the mirror, blinking his red eyes.

"Up all night with Miriam, holding her hand through her sorrows over being a failing artist. Then she cans me. Should've never trusted a dame named 'Schottland.' What the heck kind of name is that for an artist anyway? Should sign your paintings 'Mimi Schott,' I told her. Then she cans me."

He drew his razor slowly down his cheek, wincing as he took a nick.

"Why do I take on all the turkeys? Stay up all night, then wake up to a bunch of creepy kids on TV. Well—" he nicked his nose and winced again—"let 'em go to Japan if they want. Let 'em use old Philbin as a patsy to promote their stupid cause. Geez." He mimicked Tanner's high-pitched voice: "If you'll remember, viewers, this country's called America.' What a load of junk. Who cares if a bunch of crummy little kids set out on their own to arrange to play a game of ball in—"

Abruptly he stopped. He stopped shaving. He stopped breathing. He stared at his half-lathered face in the mirror, his features frozen. Then his eyes widened. He breathed out a long "whooo."

He scratched off the rest of his whiskers in seconds, pulled his tie tight, grabbed his suit jacket off the hook, and raced for the phone. "Lots of people, that's who!" He dialed quickly. "I'm sure that kid gave an address. Must have given them his phone number. If I can get to them first . . ."

The Polo Lounge in the Beverly Hills Hotel is crowded, noisy, and chic. Movie stars, moguls, jet-setters, agents, and wheeler-dealers populate the lounge. It is a good place to see and be seen by important people or, as they say, Beautiful People. It is a good place to take people whom you want to impress.

On this day, at lunchtime, the Polo Lounge was packed. Waiters and guests elbowed their way irritably around the tables and through the milling throng.

Marvin Lazar, the show biz agent fallen on rather hard times, sat at a large round table set up for a dozen people. He was the only one there—a fact that caused him to receive many hostile stares from others who envied him the space.

But he didn't mean to be alone at the table. He glanced nervously at his watch, then at the door, then at his watch again. He shuffled a sheaf of papers on the table in front of him. He drummed his fingers and shifted his silverware around.

Then they arrived. Members of the Bad News Bears straggled in. It was not just their small size that attracted amused glances from the patrons, but their style of dress, which might have been called "quaint." What they were wearing—with one exception—for this special occasion was just what they always wore: a blend of T-shirts, wrinkled windbreakers, worn and torn dungarees, and tattered sneakers. No two were clad alike, except for the one item they all shared in common: On every head was a yellow baseball cap with a white "B" stitched above the bill.

Marvin spotted them instantly, rose with a happy smile, and cheerfully waved them over.

Hands jammed in dungaree pockets, they ambled to the table and dropped into the chairs.

"Marvelous to finally meet you boys," Marvin said, slipping around the table in a belated attempt to usher each one into a seat. "Wonderful." He nodded persistently. "Welcome to show business." He grinned and looked at each of them.

The Bears seemed not even to notice him. They looked around the room with high curiosity, returning the stares they were receiving. A waiter arrived and passed out the menus with a kind of haughty elegance.

The boys snatched them from his hand and began quickly tracing their fingers over the listings of full meals and sandwiches.

"Order any and all you want," Marvin said, beaming. "Everything's on Marvin."

"Who's Marvin?" Tanner asked, not looking up from his menu.

"Why, me, of course. Old Marvin Lazar, your new friend and benefactor."

"What's a benefactor?"

"Someone who helps you, looks after you, sees to your welfare."

"We ain't on no kinda welfare," Ahmad said huffily.

"No, no, I mean—"

"He means he's paying for the grub," said Engelberg, rubbing his round belly hungrily.

All of them, with one exception, studied their menus. The one exception was the one who also dressed differently. Kelly Leak was wearing a blue blazer, open-necked paisley shirt, and tinted sunglasses. He continued to scan the room, studying the might-be and might-be-not celebrities.

Ahmad leaned over to help Rasula comprehend the menu. Engelberg's lips formed over and over again the silent words, "This and this and this and . . ." Tanner wrinkled up his nose at the selection. Rudi Stein looked cross-eyed, which is how he always looked at written material.

Rudi Stein was the team's pitcher, not because he threw well, but because he was tall and built like a beanpole and thus could use his long arms and legs to wind up impressively. He would waggle his arms over his head and kick as high as Warren Spahn. He had a different windup for every type of pitch, regardless of the fact that the pitches all came in the same way. Anything near the plate was a success. Even when batters blasted it.

The Bears did not figure primarily on strikeouts or

throwing runners out at first or ordinary catches of fly balls. They figured they had four shots at each batter: first, second, third, and home. Somewhere along the line, by some quirk of fate, they would stop the man one way or the other, and they were successful enough to win some important games.

And at bat, the Bears relied largely on the rather loose defensive play common to all small-boys' teams to get their own men on base occasionally. Sooner or later Kelly Leak would come to bat, and like as not he would blast one. From time to time—and on certain occasions of great significance in the past—that would be enough.

"Now then," Marvin said, nodding around the table, "which one of you have I been talking to on the phone? E.R.W. Tillyard the Third, I believe."

"That's me, Mr. Lazar." Tillyard pushed his glasses back up his nose and waved an index finger in the air.

"Marvin, Marvin," he said quickly. "Everybody calls me Marvin." He smiled around at the unsmiling group. "And what's your first name, E.R.W.? Edward? Edgar? Ernest? Earl? Everett?"

"I'd rather you called me Tillyard, Mr.—unh, Marvin."

"Oh." He cleared his throat. "Fine, Tillyard, fine. Dandy. Tillyard it is. Interesting name."

"Same as my father's. All of it."

"Yes, of course."

"And my grandfather's."

"Sure, naturally. The Third."

"Just call me Tillyard."

"Yes, yes. I just meant—"

"Foreign food," Tanner grumbled, wrinkling up his nose at the menu. "All foreign."

"Eggs Benedict and steak sandwiches?" Toby said. "That's foreign?"

"This is Beverly Hills, ain't it? Foreign. Ethnic. Anyway, he was a traitor to this country."

"Who?"

"That Benedict guy. Arnold Benedict. Turncoat. Probably foreign."

"That's Benedict Arnold," Tillyard corrected. "And anyway, that has nothing to do with anything. We're here on business." He turned to Lazar. "Forgive me for getting right to the point, Marvin. But you said you've already raised the money for our trip to Japan."

"Almost." Marvin was conscious of the waiter, who had long been hovering nearby and was now circling the table taking orders. He stood a long time by Engelberg, nodding and writing. "I'm involved in very serious negotiations with ABC, CBS, Mutual, and other networks over broadcasting the game. They love the idea. I'm just holding out for the best deal for all of us."

"All of us?" Tanner looked skeptical.

"Of course." Marvin ordered his third Bloody Mary. "We're in this together. But let's not talk about that right now." He held up the sheaf of papers in front of him. "Let's get the boring things out of the way first."

"Let's get eating out of the way first," said Engelberg, looking around anxiously.

"It'll be here in a sec." Marvin leaned forward, looking serious and businesslike. Most of the boys were paying attention to him. He shuffled the papers. "These are contracts. They are, in effect, an agreement between myself, as your promoter, and you."

"We already been promoted," Tanner said. "Junior high."

"Not that kind of promotion." Marvin's patience was strained slightly. "Promoting your careers. That's what I do. Sell talent. So now, listen carefully." He took a sip of his drink. "You must take these contracts home to your parents for approval. If you or your parents have any questions, don't hesitate to call me. If there are still questions, by all means have a lawyer look them over."

"Lawyers cost money," Rasula said, nodding at his older brother in appreciation of his own sophistication.

"I thought of that and, as a matter of fact, I have a particular lawyer in mind if you need him. All I'm telling you is, this is all on the up and up. Never rush into signing something that you don't understand."

Tillyard picked up a copy of the contract and leafed through it. "It'll take some study."

"Of course. Study it. Review it. Discuss it among yourselves. Where's my—" He had reached for his Bloody Mary. It was gone. "Who took my—"

"Mr. Lazar?"

He looked up at the waiter, who stood holding out a telephone. "Call for you."

"Oh yes, thanks." He answered the phone and listened. "He has to cancel again tonight, hunh? He wants tomorrow? Well, maybe *not* tomorrow! Tell him I'll call him next month sometime!" He slammed down the receiver, pleased with his assertiveness.

Food was served. The boys dug in. Marvin clasped his hands together and smiled at them.

Tillyard looked up, his mouth stuffed with steak. "Let me eat for a few minutes first. Then I've got some questions."

"Of course, of course, take your time. I'll just order another drink. Wonder who took . . . ?"

*　*　*

It was Kelly Leak. Kelly was now prowling through the Polo Lounge, Marvin's drink in his hand. Every once in a while he put the glass to his lips pretending to sip. But he did not sip, because alcohol made him sick. That was a secret he did not share with the Bears. He carried the drink because, in his view, carrying a drink made him look slick, like the coolest of the cool.

Eventually, he wound his way to the bar, where he edged in beside a very attractive dark-haired woman at least ten years older than he. He put his drink on the bar, turned slowly toward her, and narrowed his eyes to look coolly at her through his tinted glasses. "Saw you on 'Kojak.' You're pretty good."

Not responding, she took a sip of a yellow drink Kelly couldn't identify. She reached down for her purse, put it on her lap, and snapped it open.

Quickly Kelly snatched his cigarette pack out of his blazer pocket, jiggled it to shake the tips out, and held it out to her—held it right in front of her nose, in fact.

She snapped her head back, looking at the pack.

"Go ahead," Kelly said. "Take one. I got a whole 'nother pack." He waggled the cigarettes in front of her.

She shrugged and delicately removed a cigarette. She had the lighter out of her purse and the cigarette lit before Kelly could find his own lighter. Still she had not looked at him once. She tilted her head back and blew a puff of smoke out over the bar.

Kelly glanced around, enjoying what he imagined to be the envy of every other man who witnessed this conquest.

"Yeah, you're pretty good," he said smoothly, "on TV, at least." He leaned on the bar with his elbow and smiled coolly at her. "I'd never do TV myself. Too much crap on TV. Better to start out in the movies—

33

for me, at least. A sensitive role. My agent says I belong in a top sensitive role. 'Course not everybody can land a real sensitive role. You, now, I think maybe you could. I might be of some help along that line. Through my agent. Maybe if you'd just give me your name and—"

"Hi, Belinda, sorry I'm late." A big, handsome man shoved between Kelly and the woman.

"Glad you're here," she said. "I was getting worried, and—" She whispered something in the man's ear. They chuckled together and glanced at Kelly.

But Kelly was already backing away. He turned and fled through the crowd back to the table.

Tillyard wiped his mouth with a napkin, belched quietly, picked up the contract, and leaned forward toward Marvin. "It says here we each get two percent of the profits."

"Right. Easy money, and good money for you."

"Two and a half is not much."

"Pardon?"

"He's right," Engelberg put in. "We're the talent, after all."

"It should be five percent," Tillyard said.

Marvin chuckled dryly. "Five is a little unreasonable, my boy."

Miguel Aguilar had, as usual, been following the discussion with his eyes. Now he reached over and tugged Tillyard's sleeve. "*¿Quién es este hombre de* William Morris *tenemos que ver este tarde a las dos?*"

"We don't see Mr. Rosenberg until two o'clock, Miguel."

Marvin's smile faded. "Rosenberg? The William Morris Agency?"

"Yes."

34

"Well, um, you'll like him. Old friend of mine. Wonderful guy. You're, unh, going to speak to him about this, about representing you?"

The boys nodded.

Marvin flushed slightly. "Well, sure, it's a good idea. Fine, sure. You should talk to as many people as possible, of course. I just thought we . . ." His voice trailed off. He shook his head. Then he brightened. "I'll tell you, though, as great a guy as Chip Rosenberg is, this is not really his bag, this sort of thing. I'm just being honest with you, not trying to sway you toward me or anything. But he's mainly into variety acts, singers, rock and roll. He doesn't know anything about athletes."

"Well, we just thought we should talk to him," Tillyard said. "About things like what percentages he would give us."

Marvin put down his Bloody Mary and took instead a big gulp of water. "You could be right about the two and a half. We'll make it three."

"Four and a half."

Tillyard and Marvin locked eyes.

"Four," Marvin said.

"Deal." Tillyard smiled wryly. "That is, of course, pending our meeting with Mr. Rosenberg."

Tanner, suspicious from the first, had been growing more and more wary through the lunch. "Hey you!" He pointed a fork at Marvin. "Whoever you are."

"Yes?"

"What is it you really do, anyway, with this *promote* business?"

"Pardon?" Marvin looked confused.

"I mean, we know *your* name, but what's the name of your *job*?"

"I don't quite understand what—"

"Every job got a name," Ahmad said, "like doctor, lawyer, telephone man, bill collector."

"Well, unh, I've done just about everything you can think of connected with this industry."

"What industry?" Tanner asked.

"Show biz. That's what we're talking about. Movies, stage, circus—"

"Do you get people jobs, like on TV?"

"Yes, on occasion I've been able to get people on really big shows, like—"

"Which people?"

"What?"

"Which people you get jobs for?"

"You mean their names?"

"Yeah, who?"

"Well, um, mainly these days I'm producing and promoting. My only clients are, unh, a handful of close friends—that is, the ones I get jobs for, as opposed to producing and promoting. I do it for them as a favor."

"You work for William Bendix?"

"Unh, Bendix." He blinked. "William Bendix is no longer with us. He's among the departed, as we say. Why would you ask about—"

"What about John Wayne?" Tanner narrowed his eyes to slits.

Marvin cleared his throat. "Well, I know Big John. Duke, we call him."

"So call him."

"What?"

Tanner pointed to the telephone next to Marvin. "Call him. You got a phone right there, don't you? Give him a call."

A few beads of perspiration broke out on Marvin's forehead. He watched Engelberg receive two more side dishes of food. He cleared his throat. "Now wouldn't be a good time. Duke doesn't like to be bothered at certain times. Like now, for instance."

"Try."

"No good. I just remembered he's on location now. Out in the hills some place. The desert. A western they're shooting. Can't reach him. Sorry. Some other time."

Tanner snorted derisively.

Toby had been studying his copy of the contract. He traced his finger under a line. "Marvin, we're going to need three more tickets."

"Tickets?"

Rudi Stein, on his knees on the chair, leaned his lanky frame far across the table. "Yeah. See, we've done some scouting, and we've got three players already picked out. There's this one kid up in Fresno, and another one—"

"No!" Marvin shook his head violently. "No, no, absolutely not. No ringers. No special players added on now. You play as you are. The regular Bad News Bears. That's it." He thumped a fist lightly on the table. "You must understand, you are the *underdogs*. That's the important thing. That's what attracted me in the first place. That's what pulled me away from my busy schedule to work with you guys. Everybody roots for the underdog." His face reddened as he got worked up. "That's how we get people interested in the game! Underdogs! That's what makes it a profitable enterprise!"

He banged his fist on the table again, harder this time, making the silverware jump. He paused for a moment, the Bears' wide eyes riveted on him. He softened his voice a notch. "Did you guys see *Rocky*, the movie about the boxer? Big hit. Enormous. Why?

He was the underdog. Believe me, I know this business. We're going to have everybody in this country rooting for you. And that's what I'm after—we're *all* after."

He let his words sink in.

Ahmad spoke in a low voice. "But those dudes over there are *bad*, man. I mean really baaad. We'll get wiped out, 'less we take on some—"

"So what?" Marvin grinned. "So what?"

The table lapsed into a silence. Engelberg even stopped eating. They all looked at him.

"Well," Marvin waved his hand, "don't be so darned negative anyway. Maybe you'll win." He looked around at the stony faces. "Blast it, you *will* win. Or come close, at least. It's all the same. You'll be underdogs, in any case."

Tanner rose slowly from his chair and came around the table to Marvin. He grabbed the large chain around Marvin's neck and gave it a quick twist. "Look, you crud," he growled, "we ain't traveling no thousands of miles to get our behinds stomped by no foreign ball team. You don't have to tell us we're gonna win or come close. We know what we're gonna do."

Tillyard and Ahmad pulled Tanner away.

Marvin straightened out his chain and rubbed his neck, eyeing Tanner with disbelief. "Are you for real, kid?"

Tanner stood glaring at him.

"Well, we've got that two o'clock appointment, Marvin," Tillyard said, "so we better go. Thanks for lunch."

The other Bears got up and mumbled their thanks.

"I'll give you a call," Tillyard said, "after we've gone over these contracts and made our choice." He steered

38

Tanner toward the door, the other Bears falling into line behind. "Stick by your phone."

The waiter graciously presented the check to Marvin.

Marvin looked at it, and his mouth dropped open. "One hundred and seventy-six dollars and seventy-eight cents! What the—"

"And by the way"—Tillyard had left the Bears and come back—"you better start working on the Miguel Aguilar problem. He's an illegal alien and it's going to be tough to get him out of the country, into Japan, and back into this country."

Marvin continued to stare at the check. "How do we get nineteen meals when we were only eleven people?" Then his head snapped up. "Illegal alien?"

The Bears were gone.

"Illegal alien?" he muttered in a daze. "One hundred and seventy-six dollars and seventy-eight cents for an illegal alien?" Still dazed, he signed the check, "Illegal Alien," and walked out.

THREE

It would take some doing, no doubt about it. But Marvin was an old hand at doing things that took some doing. Especially things that took some slick, sleight-of-hand financial doing. For example, Marvin had little money but several credit cards. He was already in debt almost up to the limit on each card. But he played his credit cards like a Las Vegas dealer.

He strode confidently up to the ticket counter at a Japan Airlines travel agency and beckoned regally to a clerk. "Tokyo, sir. One ticket, if you please. And put it on my Diner's Club card, if you would be so kind. Hope it's a good flight. I go to Tokyo about once a week, on business, important business. Last flight was delayed. Botched up some very important business for me."

"So sorry, sir." The clerk bowed humbly, accepted the credit card, ran the ticket through the machine, and presented it to him, with the card. "I hope this flight is more satisfactory."

"We both hope so. Thank you."

A block away, Marvin strode just as confidently into another travel agency where he made a similar announcement, except that this time he directed the clerk to put it on American Express.

The agent looked at the card. "This ticket is over a

thousand dollars," he said meekly. "I'll have to call for authorization."

"Then just make it a one-way ticket," Marvin said gruffly. "I'm in a hurry and have no time for such nonsense. I'll get the return ticket in Tokyo."

"Yes, sir, as you wish." And the clerk ran the ticket through the machine and handed it to him, with the American Express card.

In just such a fashion did Marvin visit several more travel agencies, until he had at last assembled a wide variety of tickets stamped with a wide variety of credit cards. He had not been able quite to achieve exactly what he had in mind. All tickets had in common the final destination, but the routes varied as widely as the tickets themselves. What he had left to do was somehow to distill the wide variety of tickets and wide variety of routes into a single program that would carry him and all the Bears to Tokyo together.

But that was the easy part. Marvin knew that once you had the tickets in hand, it was a simple matter to exchange them. And so he would simply go to the ticket counter at the airport and have a clerk redesign the itinerary to get him and his new clients aboard the same plane.

The meeting with Mr. Rosenberg at the William Morris Agency—one of the largest and most prestigious talent agencies in the world—had not gone the way William Morris people were used to. The Bears were never easily awed, certainly not by people in suits and ties, not even leisure suits. Rosenberg had carried on for a while about putting out special Bears' T-shirts and posters, and lining up commercial endorsements for Disneyland and California oranges. He never said anything about playing baseball.

Finally Tanner had risen and, speaking for the group, interrupted Rosenberg's spiel to say, "We ain't signing nothin' that ain't a paper saying we're going to Japan to beat them foreigners to a pulp!"

Whereupon the Bears had stalked out.

The next day, Marvin Lazar called to tell them he had already arranged for their flight to Japan, and that they should see about getting passport pictures taken immediately.

So Marvin was elected their promoter, and it was cause for celebration. The Bears celebrated by drinking a punch bowl full of their special concoction of Coke, root beer, apple cider, and quinine water—the last ingredient added because of their giddily wicked assumption that quinine water had something like alcohol in it.

Their celebrative mood continued all the way to the passport photo shop, a small, dark office on the ground floor of a building that also housed a donut shop—where they would lunch. Marvin joined them to oversee the operation.

The photographer patiently arranged each boy in turn, seeming oblivious to their chatter and behavior.

Jimmy Feldman sat stiffly and grinned at the camera. Rudi Stein kept combing and recombing his straight, black hair until Marvin finally snatched the comb away and shoved him down into the chair.

Engelberg giggled and waved, then started to make an obscene gesture at the camera, when Marvin slapped his hand down. Engelberg's photo showed him in a pout.

Kelly turned his head for a profile shot.

"This ain't a bust, Kelly," Ahmad said.

"Oh yeah." He turned to face the camera, smiling coolly.

Rasula grinned broadly, but somehow the photo caught him with his eyes closed.

Tanner stared icily at the camera, like a boxer eyeing an opponent before the opening bell.

Miguel Aguilar smiled toward the camera, but kept his eyes averted up toward Marvin, so his passport photo showed only the whites of his eyes.

At last the great day of departure arrived, and the Bears assembled at the vast Los Angeles International Airport. Marvin had all he could do to keep them together, as they wandered off this way and that to see planes landing and taking off, travelers milling at ticket counters and car-rental agencies.

For a time, Tanner refused to leave the Hertz counter. "I'm waitin' for O.J. Simpson," he told Marvin, in resisting pleas to join the team. "He's bound to come running through here any minute."

"That's just a TV commercial," Marvin said.

"I ain't prejudiced," Tanner said.

Finally they managed to check their luggage through and join the line going past the security check with carry-on bags. The bags were opened, guards rifled the contents, and passed them on. Except for Tanner's. The guard reached into his army-surplus duffel bag and pulled out a plastic submachine gun.

"What's this?" he asked.

"What's it look like?" Tanner said. "It ain't even loaded."

"Things like this make us nervous," the guard said, "even if it is a toy."

"It ain't a toy," Tanner said angrily. "It's a practice gun. I'm gonna use it to—"

"For heaven's sake!" Marvin exclaimed as he pushed Tanner away. "We're late as it is! Please pass these boys through, mister," he said to the guard.

43

The guard insisted on having Tanner's gun packaged separately and sent through with the shipped luggage. Marvin managed to restrain Tanner, who wanted to settle the matter with the guard right then and there with fists, and got him and the rest of the Bears through the line and onto the plane.

The Japan Airlines DC-10 lifted off and headed west, which is the direction people in California go to get to the Far East.

Marvin was already exhausted. He slumped into a seat next to Tillyard.

"Relax," Tillyard said. "Everything's going to be fine. I even took care of the hotel reservations for you."

"What do you mean?" Marvin sat up straight. "I already made reservations."

"I know. I changed them. We have a more appropriate place now, more Japanese."

"But I had us all set up at the Hilton!"

"You can stay at Hiltons anywhere," Tillyard said calmly. "There are cultural aspects to this trip as well as business, Marvin."

"Oh my." Marvin sighed and sagged back in the seat. "What's the name of the place?"

"I don't know. But it's supposed to be very Oriental."

Marvin looked severely pained. "Well, just so they got bathrooms and plenty of phones."

Tillyard stared straight ahead.

"They do, don't they?"

"Very Oriental."

Marvin closed his eyes.

Kelly and Feldman sat together. A Japanese stewardess served them Cokes. When she was gone, Kelly reached into his bag and pulled out a small rum flask. The flask was filled with leftover punch from their earlier celebration. He poured some punch into the Coke and took a long drink.

He and Feldman had been listening to music through the headphones provided by the airline. Feldman saw Kelly with the rum flask, and, thinking it had rum in it, was disturbed. He pulled off the earphones. "Hey, Kelly."

Kelly continued listening sleepily to the music.

Feldman pulled Kelly's earphones off his ears. "Kelly?" Kelly frowned. "A lot of us are worried about you, you know. Here you are drinking. I know you think it's corny, but no one with problems is alone in this world. He's always there to help and comfort and guide—"

"Can it!" Kelly snatched his earphones back. "Ever since you started with that stuff, you've been a royal pain. Let a man drink in peace. Get off my case and go sit somewhere else, before I move you myself!" He took another swig of harmless punch, winced as if rum were burning down his throat, and put the earphones back on.

Feldman, hurt, left for another seat.

Farther back in the tourist-class cabin, Rudi Stein moaned in his seat. Nausea welled up in him. Everytime he opened his eyes to look out the window, it was worse. But he couldn't resist looking out the window. He tried to will the sickness away.

Tillyard had walked up and down the aisle gathering all the passports for what he called "inspection." Now he sat back down in his seat and flipped through them. "Marvin, there's a big mistake here on Miguel's passport."

"Hmm?" Marvin, who had been dreaming about Marge, his unseen answering-service woman, sat up and rubbed his eyes.

"It says here his name is Miguel Aguilar Lazar."

"Miguel? Oh yeah. It's okay. I got his ticket on family plan. He's traveling as my nephew."

Toby Whitewood leaned across the aisle. "Miguel's your nephew?"

"For now, for now." Marvin heard groans coming from the rear. He got up and headed back.

Rudi writhed in his seat, alternately looking out the window and closing his eyes.

"Air sickness, hunh?" Marvin patted his head. "No big deal, Stein." He pulled out the plastic-coated bag from the seat-back pouch and opened it directly in front of Rudi's mouth. "It may surprise you, Stein, but this here was designed specifically for this particular illness." He patted him again and smiled. "It'll pass. All things pass, in time."

"Ooooh." Rudi took the bag and leaned over it.

Marvin turned to Rasula, seated next to Rudi, smiled at him and tweaked his nose. "They're gonna love that face in Japan, kid. Gonna love it!"

Rasula grinned shyly and watched Marvin retreat back up the aisle.

Ahmad's eyes followed Marvin coldly.

"Why they gonna love my face?" Rasula asked.

Ahmad snarled, "'Cause everybody everywhere loves faces like ours, Little Bro. Didn't you know that?"

"No. I like Marvin."

"Well, don't get to likin' him too much."

"Why not?"

"It ain't healthy."

"What's that got to do with my health?"

"Plenty, on this trip. And he ain't no good, that's why."

46

"He *seems* good."

"Lot of folks *seem*. You listen to Big Bro, now. You got too much like in you sometimes."

"Man can't have too much like."

"A *boy* can. You just be careful. Key on me, okay?"

"Okay."

Some Bears gathered around Marvin at his seat, asking questions.

"I still don't understand where you came up with it," Toby said.

"I told you," Marvin said, sighing. "I paid for the tickets with the advance I got from Spalding. They're interested in promoting their sporting equipment."

"That's a pretty rich company," Engelberg said. "If they paid, how come we couldn't go first class then?"

"I never go first class. It's a ripoff. All snobs up there. Intellectual wasteland. People removed from the mainstream. You guys want to be with the snobs?"

"Yeah," Engelberg said.

"Why couldn't we have at least gone nonstop?" Toby whined.

"Yeah," Tillyard said, leafing through his tickets. "We're going to be on planes for the next day and a half. Six stopovers and four different connections."

"Listen, be happy we're all going to be together the whole trip. That took some doing. So many flights booked solid."

"Yeah, but Air Icelandic? Borneo Airways?"

"You're going to Japan, aren't you?" Marvin said irritably. "Have some gratitude. A few days ago you weren't going anyplace. So relax. Think about the game."

"Wonder what we get to eat on Borneo Airways," Engelberg mused.

"Probably a missionary," Toby said.

"Everybody go sit down," Marvin directed. "Get some rest."

Kelly, now sitting alone, sipped his drink and stared out the window, immersed in a mood which seemed to blacken with the passing minutes. His teammates recognized those times when Kelly was getting into a mood, and avoided him.

After a while the movie screen at the head of the cabin lit up. The movie was *Rocky*, the story of a down-and-out mediocre fighter who managed to land a title bout with the champ.

Marvin jumped to his feet and turned to address the group. "All right, you guys. This is one of the reasons I chose this flight. I want everybody to see this movie. You understand me? Study it. Identify with the main character."

"Geez," Engelberg groaned, "sounds like we're gonna have to write a report or something."

"Just watch it closely. I mean it." Marvin sat back down.

Some Bears bustled around behind him as the main titles appeared on the screen.

Suddenly a baseball blasted into the screen and knocked it sideways.

Tanner came running up the aisle to retrieve the ball. "Not so hard, Engelberg, you crud!"

Marvin sprang to his feet. "What in blazes is going on?"

Heads throughout the cabin were turned toward the rear, where Engelberg was holding a bat. Curses and mutterings came from several tourists' seats.

Marvin loped back to Engelberg. "What in blazes are you doing?"

"Playing baseball," Tanner said, elbowing Marvin

away. "Practicing. This ain't no vacation, you know."

A stewardess wrestled the screen back into position.

Marvin, flushed with embarrassment and anger, grabbed the ball from Tanner, slapped his hand away, and pushed him toward a seat. "You guys sit back down this instant and watch this movie!" he whispered loudly.

"What for?" Tanner said, stumbling from Marvin's push. "I already saw it. It stinks. The bum loses the fight."

The Bears watched the movie.

The rest of their trip passed in what the Bears would remember only as a foggy, two-day dream of weary plodding, restless sitting, interrupted naps, a mish-mash of food and locales and landings and takings-off. For Marvin, the fortunate part was that the boys were so tired that they had no energy left for further mischief or difficult questions.

Coach Shimizu sat behind the wheel of his station wagon fighting the traffic on a crowded Tokyo boulevard. To look at him, one would not know he was fighting traffic because, as usual, his expression was rigidly unemotional.

Crammed in beside and behind him were the members of his baseball team, all dressed in identical gray blazers and blue shorts. The boy sitting nearest him squirmed to reach the radio, turning it on to a station playing American rock. Shimizu impassively and immediately turned it off.

"I'll bet they wouldn't come to the airport to meet us," said a boy in the back, "if we went to the United States."

"Whatever the truth of that is," Shimizu said, "we cannot know. It is true that Americans are not primarily noted for good manners—at least not those manners we are used to in our exchanges. But that does not change our manners. We shall be as polite and hospitable as possible."

One of the boys in the back nudged his comrades to either side and snickered softly. He leaned forward. "Coach, tell us about the time you had lunch with the Emperor."

A couple of boys groaned quietly. Others snickered expectantly at yet another recital of the tale.

"Yeah," said one, "about the time when his brother-in-law introduced you."

"Oh, now—" Shimizu showed the slightest of smiles and humbly demurred. "Boys, we've been through this so many times. I'm sure you're bored by now." He loved to talk about it, of course—about the meeting, about the old days in general, when respect was shown, when things Japanese were not intruded upon by things American. But he knew that these boys, growing up in different times, would not truly understand his feelings. Still—

"Please, please," begged one of the boys, hiding a smile behind his hand, "tell us. It's very interesting."

One of the boys was not pleased by this secret sarcasm. "Cool it," he grumbled.

A couple of others jabbed him in the ribs, as if warning him not to spoil their fun.

"What did you talk about?" persisted one.

"Yes," crooned another. "He's a great man, isn't he, the Emperor?"

"Well, it's true he is a great man," Shimizu said carefully, "by my standards, at least. And it's true, of course, that I did meet him on that occasion—"

A fight had broken out in the back between the boy who resisted the teasing and one of those who teased.

Shimizu pulled the station wagon to the curb, turned around, and, with very few words and one harsh, authoritative glare, stopped the struggle.

"I think it would be well," he said, upon resuming the drive to the airport, "for you all to keep in mind where we are going, and why, and how our country expects you to behave."

A four-propeller aircraft with Arabic lettering on the fuselage thumped onto the runway and taxied over to the exit ramp. Passengers lined up quickly to file out.

Among the Bears' weary ensemble, only Marvin looked spry and awake.

"All right, boys," he said, waving them together, "let's try and look our best. The welcoming committee may have some questions. Probably be some important press people there."

Tanner quickly ducked into the lavatory with his duffel bag. Kelly, who had kept himself awake through most of the trip by concentrating on being moody, was now sound asleep as if out cold.

Marvin reached Rudi Stein's seat, smiled at the pale pitcher, and helped him to his feet. "I knew you'd make it, Stein. All things pass."

"I passed a lot," Rudi said weakly. He suddenly coughed violently, flecking Marvin's white shirt with bits of a sandwich he had recently tried to chew.

Marvin stared at him blankly, wiping some bits off his golden necklace.

"You shouldn't have lifted me up so fast," Rudi said.

"You're right about that, Stein," Marvin said, looking with dismay at his stained shirt. "You're very right about that."

"All things pass," Stein said.

51

"Mmm."

As the passengers filed through Customs, Marvin tried to pull his jacket closed over his stained shirt with one hand while he steadied the groggy Stein with the other.

Kelly, trying to wake up, was being supported on either side by Feldman and Ahmad.

Strange sights and sounds and smells affronted their senses. They stared around at all the Japanese people and products and signs and shops.

Marvin searched the terminal for signs of a reception party, expecting banners and perhaps a band. Finally his eyes brightened as he saw the neatly regimented row of boys and Coach Shimizu. Beside them stood half a dozen members of the print media, identifiable by their notebooks and poised pencils.

Marvin was all smiles as he headed for them. He reached out to take Coach Shimizu's extended hand and shook it vigorously. A translator stepped forward and bowed. Shimizu gestured to his row of boys, and all bowed to Marvin, who bowed back.

"Fine group of boys you've got here," Marvin said, enunciating carefully for the translator. "Marvelous group. So polite. You must be Coach Shee, um, Shee—"

"Shimizu," the coach said softly, bowing again.

"Right. Lazar. Marvin Lazar here. Forgive the way I look." He glanced down at his spattered shirt. "An accident. Could happen to anybody."

The translator passed on the words to Shimizu, then motioned toward the press.

"Oh yes." Marvin put an arm around Shimizu's shoulders and tugged him along. "They'll want some good quotes, of course. They'll find us very cooperative. Yes, sir. Couple of the boys are tired. A long flight. Away from home and all that. So I'll take care of the introductions."

As the Bears remained facing the Far Eastern Champions, sizing up their competition, Marvin eagerly shook hands with the members of the press. "Real pleased to be here. Game's going to be great. Marvelous. Good for both marvelous countries. Sportsmanship, that's what it's all about. Good lesson for the entire world . . ."

At the Customs counter, meanwhile, a shiny helmet glistened among the crowd. It was on the small head of Tanner Boyle. That was not all he had put on when he slipped into the men's room before deplaning. He had also changed into battle fatigues and army combat boots several sizes too large.

The Customs official lowered his glasses and peered over them at the scowling face under the helmet.

Tanner slapped his passport down on the counter. "Just pass me through, mister. Everything's legal. I'm American. My picture's on it right there."

The official smiled as he stamped the passport and handed it back.

Marvin handed out prepared press releases to the reporters. They were several pages long, and included brief biographical sketches of each of the Bears, along with an expanded account of his own career. "Just some things I had written up for you gentlemen from the fourth estate—to make it easier for you. A little information about us. I know your countrymen have a lot of curiosity." He looked around. "No TV news here, hunh? Strange. But I suppose you fellows do things a little differently here. . . ."

Tanner stormed up to the two lines of young ballplayers. He stalked between the lines, eyeing the Japanese boys as if reviewing prisoners of war. The host boys glanced at each other.

Tanner came to a stop in front of the boy who had earlier tried to stop his teammates from teasing their coach. The boy had a scowl matching Tanner's. Arm clasped behind his back, jaw out, Tanner glared at him. They were about the same size.

"Short pants, hunh?" Tanner sneered. "Funny clothes for whale killers." Tanner was recalling a recent TV show about Japanese fishing fleets hunting whales.

The boy took a deep breath. So did Tanner. Then they lunged at each other, grabbed each other like wrestlers, and tumbled to the floor.

Shimizu and Marvin scampered over to pull them apart.

"What happened?" Marvin looked with embarrassment at the crowd that gathered quickly to watch. "Where'd those clothes come from, Tanner?"

"Viet Nam," Tanner hissed proudly, his fists clenched at his sides.

"Well, this is no war, and we're not an army. Come on, you guys"—he motioned for the Bears to follow him over to the press—"let's get 'em a good team photo."

He yanked Kelly's shoulder. "Wake up, Leak! What's the matter with you?"

Kelly blinked several times and tried to focus. Marvin pushed him into line with the rest. "Big smiles, boys. California smiles." Flashbulbs went off. "Once more, now." The photographers, who had started away, politely stopped and took several more shots.

Outside the terminal, a Datsun van was waiting at the curb for the Bears to board.

Tanner pulled back. "Foreign," he growled. "Everything's foreign here. The people are all foreign."

"Since this is Japan," Tillyard said, "it's actually *we* who are the foreigners here."

"I ain't no foreigner! Foreigners ain't what made our country great!"

"I'm afraid you're mistaken there." Tillyard raised an index finger into the air. "You see, our whole country was originally populated by—"

"Come on, boys," Marvin called, "into the truck."

"I ain't goin' nowhere in no cheap, tin-can Japanmobile!" Tanner shouted.

The rest of the Bears squeezed into the van while the driver piled their luggage on top. The motor was running.

Tanner sat stiffly on a bus bench on the sidewalk, his arms folded defiantly across his chest.

"Hey, Tanner," Marvin said, walking over and trying to remain calm, chuckling, "maybe you'd prefer a Chevy, hunh?"

"Ford'll do. Pontiac. Harley-Davidson."

Marvin reached for him. Tanner slid away and hopped behind the bench.

"You crazy little—" Marvin tried to keep his voice low.

The Bears called from the bus, begging Tanner to end his holdout and think about the game.

"I'll go on only one condition," Tanner said finally.

FOUR

Through the sardine-like mash of traffic and the heavy haze of smog, the Datsun van rolled along with its contents of Bears. It would not have attracted much attention but for the fulfillment of Tanner's "condition." A large American flag extended out the window from Tanner's hands and blew in the wind.

They arrived at a low and starkly designed hotel. They all marched in to be greeted by a loud "gong" and the smiling faces of two female attendants dressed in splendid, bright kimonos. The women bowed deeply and led them up a flight of stairs to their suite.

At the door, the women stepped out of their clogs, and gestured for the boys to similarly remove their footwear before entering. All flopped down in the hallway to pull off their shoes.

All except Tanner. Disregarding the ancient custom and the current hospitality, he stalked into the room wearing his army boots and holding onto the flag.

Marvin grabbed him by the shirt collar and pulled him back out.

The boys shuffled in on stocking feet and milled around to look at everything with curiosity. The suite was comprised of three rooms partitioned from each other by thin sliding screens. Woven mats covered portions of the floor. There were no chairs or beds. By Western standards, the suite was virtually bare.

"Very Oriental," Tillyard said, nodding.

"You booked us into a darned vacant lot, Tillyard," Marvin said. "An airplane hangar. Where are all the phones?"

Tillyard shrugged.

Followed closely by Rasula, who never allowed himself to be separated more than a couple of feet from him, Marvin vainly searched the rooms for a phone.

He went out and down to the front desk, still dogged by Rasula. He finally found a clerk that could understand him, and complained about the lack of even a single telephone.

"I'm a three-phone guy," he said, trying to make his protest as polite as possible, even though he considered phones the most important thing in the world. "I'm dead without phones. At least three."

The clerk bowed and nodded incessantly, listening.

"So can I have them? Huh? And sir, is it too much to ask, at these prices, that we have furnished rooms? You know, chairs and tables and lamps and all that? Will you take care of it for me? Huh? I'll make it worth your while."

The clerk continued bowing and nodding, adding a smile when Marvin at last finished.

Marvin headed back toward the suite, Rasula placing his feet exactly in the places Marvin had placed his.

Tanner squatted outside the door. "The only way these boots come off," he said, covering them with his hands, "is when I'm dead."

"Fine," Marvin said, brushing past him. "You sleep outside for the next few days." He added, mumbling, "Ungrateful little twerp."

Then he smacked his head into the low-slung door-frame. Rasula bumped into his back.

Marvin muttered several things, while rubbing his head, bending over, and stepping through.

A girl arrived carrying a small, steaming pot. She poured ceremonial tea for the new arrivals. Marvin explained to them what tea was, and the significance of it in the Far East.

And not long thereafter, two bellhops arrived carrying three extension phones, which they quickly plugged into the sockets.

Marvin flopped down on the floor (next to Kelly, who was out cold in slumber) and snatched up the receiver and dialed the front desk. "I just want to make sure everything's understood about billing procedures. . . . No, I want the hotel bill on Diner's Club. . . . No, no, just the room bill. The phone goes on BankAmericard. Extras go on American Express . . . American Express, for heaven's sake!" He looked around. "Tillyard! Get over here, get on the phone. I don't even think he's speaking Japanese. Sounds more like Italian."

He shoved the receiver into Tillyard's hand and got up to pace around the room. "Hey, you fellows!" he called to the bellhops who were just going out. "Can you get me a *chair?* A stool? Anything, for crying out loud!"

They bowed and nodded and hurried out.

Marvin turned to pace into the next room and whacked his head again on the low beam. Grabbing his forehead, he spun away and tripped over Rasula. "Stop following me, Rasula! You're going to get us both killed!"

Rasula ran over to his brother, who hugged him.

"You just mind who you be yelling at, Marvin," Ahmad said.

"Sorry, sorry. Okay. I didn't mean it. But he's like a squirrel around my feet." He waved to Rasula. "Sorry, old buddy, didn't mean it. It's okay. Let's eat."

Engelberg, who had been dozing while sitting on the floor, suddenly awoke. "Eat? When? Where? Who?"

Marvin ordered up sandwiches, specifying "clubs," which he thought would have something in them for everybody.

The boys munched their sandwiches while Marvin huddled in a corner of the main room making phone calls. Several boys gazed out the window. It was dusk. Signs with Japanese lettering glittered in the twilight. Below their room and shadowed by adjacent towering buildings was a small, ill-kept park, with scrubby grass here and there. A game was in progress on the dirt baseball field.

"Those guys don't look so hot," Engelberg said, a wad of sandwich in his cheek.

"They're not the ones we'll be playing," Stein said.

"I don't care. I'm not impressed."

"You sound like Tanner."

"Where is he, anyway?"

"Still out in the hall. He's just sitting out there waving that big old American flag and keeping his big old boots on."

Marvin sat on his suitcase looking through his private phone book. Resula played with the buckle of one of Marvin's shoes. Feldman was reading aloud from the New Testament.

"Feldman," Marvin said, rubbing his grumbling belly, "will you please hold off on that? I promise you, the Bible when I get time. We all will. Rasula, [a] favor and put that shoe back with the other one before you get it all smudged. And get me some Tums out of my jacket."

Rasula happily skipped over to the closet.

Two young women appeared at the door, bowed, and delivered quiltlike bedclothing.

"Wow," Toby said, widening his eyes. "Are those our beds?"

"Sleeping bags," Marvin grumbled. "Now it's a camping trip all of a sudden."

"Actually, these are *futons*," Tillyard said. "They're really very practical, much less bother than all those blankets we're used to."

"Enough already with the lectures, Tillyard." Marvin picked up the phone again. "We're moving right out of this joint as soon as I get things set up." Into the phone he tried to speak Japanese. "Mashi, Mashi—"

Later that night, Marvin was still busy on the phone. Several of the boys were playing pepper, tossing and batting a ball back and forth among them.

Marvin finally got his call through. "I've got great news, Mr. Deak. ABC, who's here to cover the rematch between Ali and the Japanese wrestler Inoki, is going to broadcast the game on the twenty-first. . . ."

"Since when?" Tillyard said from across the room.

Marvin cupped his hand over the receiver, shushed Tillyard, and motioned for him to pick up a free phone. "See how my call to Voit is coming," he whispered.

Back on his phone, he said, "We're still quibbling over little things like whether they're going to do it live or on tape, but it's virtually set—whenever I give the okay. We're playing a practice inning tomorrow for the press. Big shindig. It's like the Super Bowl to these people over here. . . ."

A batted ball whizzed by his head. Marvin ducked. "Yes, Mr. Deak, we still want very much to endorse your equipment, but you're going to have to move fast. The prices have changed, on our end. Because Voit and Wilson Sporting Goods have jumped into the bidding. . . . Right, and—"

The ball thumped into Marvin's back. He slapped his hand over the receiver. "This ain't Yankee Stadium, you twerps! It's three-thirty in the morning! Will you go to sleep already? We got a big exhibition inning tomorrow!"

One by one the Bears dropped out of the pepper game and other activities and crawled into the quilts to sleep. Marvin continued telephoning, pacing around the room.

". . . Yes, Mr. Rahim, just called to tell you everything's dandy. Your boys are fine. Everybody's treating them like princes here. . . ."

He dragged the phone over to the door to the suite and peered out into the hallway. Tanner had fallen asleep against the wall, curled up with the flag.

". . . No, Mrs. Engelberg, he's not nervous at all. He's fine. . . . Oh yes, the food's excellent here. He's been saying so himself. . . . I'm sure he's had a movement, but I'll ask again in the morning. . . ."

He scooped Tanner up under one arm and lugged him back into the room, smacking his head into the beam in the process.

Gritting his teeth, he continued his calls. ". . . You're his sister? Well, I just called to say Tanner's fine, he's . . . Pardon? Well, *I* care, that's who. . . ."

* * *

Marvin was dressed, carefully groomed, and out early in the morning. When he returned cheerily to the suite, he had a bundle of newspapers under one arm and a large box of aftershave in one hand.

The Bears were cuddled in their *futons,* snoring loudly.

Marvin put the papers down and clapped his hands. "Come on, ballplayers, look alive! Up and at 'em! Big day ahead of us! Look sharp! Feel sharp! *Be* sharp!"

Groans came from reluctant Bears. Marvin tugged at them and rolled them from one side to the other. "This'll perk you all up." He opened the bottle of aftershave and began slapping it on their faces.

"Thanks," Engelberg said, sitting up, "I needed that."

When all the Bears were roused, Marvin excitedly opened one of the newspapers. "Look at this, guys! Things are beginning to roll. Especially for you. Marvin's a good old promoter, that's a fact."

He prodded Tanner into a sitting position and pointed to a photograph in the paper. Pictured were Tanner and his Japanese combatant fighting at the airport. Other Bears gathered around to look at the paper.

"You got a nose for publicity, Tanner, old sport. You had me fooled."

Tanner's eyes started to close, and Marvin slapped him with aftershave.

"Only page twelve," Kelly said.

Marvin slapped Kelly's cheeks with aftershave. "Just a start, my boy, just a start. Page one is just around the corner. Ahmad, what're you doing?"

"Just waking up Little Bro, that's all."

"By hanging him upside down from the heels?"

"Only way to get him started."

"Well, we're started, all of us." Marvin chuckled. "Come on, get spruced up. We got breakfast with the Far Eastern champs."

The teams, in uniform, sat at either side of a long table facing each other as breakfast was served. The opposing sides regarded each other with some uncertainty, for the most part avoiding any direct eye contact.

Marvin stood with Shimizu at the head of the table, taking in the scene. "Great, hunh, Shmato? Look at 'em. As comfortable together as if they'd known each other all their lives. Great lesson in this for the United Nations." He looked around the hotel's small banquet room. "Should be a cameraman or two here though, hunh? Great opportunity they're missing."

Shimizu nodded, but his face showed neither agreement nor disagreement. He did not look at Marvin.

The two sat down at a side table, joined by Tillyard, who served as a minor-league interpreter of sorts.

A glass of beer was placed at Marvin's plate. He hoisted it as a toast. "Here's to it. Don't usually drink beer in the morning, but this is a special occasion." Coach Shimizu blinked at him. "Hey, Tillyard, tell him he looks just like a Japanese actor. Pick out some famous one. Or better yet, just tell him he looks like a lot of Japanese actors. They all look pretty much the same anyway."

Tillyard did his best. Shimizu answered briefly.

"I think he said you look just like Clint Eastwood," Tillyard said. "Or maybe like a lot of American actors."

"Really?" Marvin beamed. "First time anybody said that."

Breakfast was not going smoothly for the Bears.

They had been given only chopsticks to eat with, and were fumbling miserably. Their discomfort was heightened by the fact that the boys opposite them were eating swiftly and efficiently.

Marvin pulled a document out of his sportsjacket pocket. He tapped it on the table. "Tillyard, tell him that this is a standard contract, accepted the world over. No gimmicks or fine print. Say it mainly states that I get the rights to the U.S.A., Canada, South America, and Japan."

"Japan?"

"Right. But stress that he gets the entire—and get that word right, Tillyard—the *entire* rest of the world. He gets Sweden, England, New Zealand, and Zambia. Plus all of China, Russia, and the rest."

Tillyard cleared his throat and did his best.

Tanner was growing increasingly disgusted by his inability to eat. Rice was scattered all around his bowl. He gripped one chopstick in either fist and tried to eat as if he were knitting. He glanced at his opposite across the table and saw him whipping down the food while staring back.

Tillyard finally managed to deliver what he hoped was the gist of Marvin's explanation, and now listened to the quick reply from Coach Shimizu.

He looked at Marvin and cleared his throat. "He either said it sounds great to him, or please pass the rice."

Marvin clenched his teeth. "Tillyard, you don't know diddle about the Japanese, do you? Them *or* their language. Pushovers. This could be like taking candy from a baby."

"Let's not get overly uptight, Marvin," Tillyard said, jabbing an index finger into the air.

"Got to get a real interpreter," Marvin muttered, looking around.

Engelberg gave up on the chopsticks. Not just because he couldn't handle them, but because he was always prepared for emergencies, where food was involved. From his back pocket he took a collapsible tin fork, snapped the handle straight, and dug in.

Tanner, too, gave up. He tossed the chopsticks aside and plunged his hand into the bowl of rice. He crammed a fistful into his mouth and chewed loudly.

A couple of Japanese boys giggled, which was a mistake.

Marvin was still trying to get through to Shimizu. "Listen, tell him I'll be handling all the negotiations personally, just to make sure everybody's rights are protected on both sides. But tell him we've got to work together to make this a successful venture."

Tillyard pulled out a phrase book.

Suddenly some plates crashed to the floor. Tanner and his counterpart grabbed at each other across the table. Marvin and Shimizu raced over to break it up. Shimizu scolded his boy severely while Marvin dusted rice off Tanner.

"If you're going to fight," Marvin said softly, "at least wait until there are photographers around."

In the small baseball stadium, the two teams lined up for pictures—the Bears along the first-base line, the Japanese strung out near third. A handful of press walked around. The Japanese boys were bright and alert; the Bears looked exhausted and bedraggled.

Marvin passed in front of his team, examining them. He took Rasula by the shoulders and moved him out in front. "You got to stick out more, Rasula. You're a big item."

"Just what do you mean by that?" Ahmad asked suspiciously.

Marvin chucked Rasula under the chin admiringly and stepped back to look at him. "The kisser on that kid, Ahmad. He's a heartbreaker. Trust me. Your brother is going to wow these people. You guys are going to be rich men."

He continued moving down the row tending to last-minute adjustments. He pulled Kelly's shirttail out.

"What the—"

"Got to look sloppy," Marvin said, continuing down the row. He cocked hats sideways, pushed socks down, untied some of their shoes. "Got to look a little raw. I know what I'm doing. Underdogs. That's the key. Did Rocky wear fancy suits? Darned right he didn't. He looked like an unmade bed. Sloppy."

Coach Shimizu was surrounded by a group of reporters. Though remaining cautious and reserved, clearly he enjoyed the attention. He answered all questions politely, bowing to each reporter who addressed him. None of the Bears—with the possible exception of Tillyard, once in a while—understood what Shimizu was saying, which was that his opponents were indeed worthy, and that they all looked forward to the upcoming game. He modestly shrugged off the compliments and congratulations for his having built a championship team.

Seeing that the press weren't going to question him just yet, Marvin drifted over to the dugout, where a man sat wearing a dark blazer with an ABC emblem on the pocket. The man seemed unmoved by what was going on.

"I imagine you'll be beaming the game back direct," Marvin said, smiling, "savvy as you guys are about commercial marketing."

"Live is totally out of the question, Lazar," the man said, carefully patting his neatly combed blond hair.

"What are you talking about?" Marvin sat down beside him. "We can play the game at three-thirty in the morning Tokyo time. So it'll go on opposite NBC's 'Game of the Week.' And you'll kill 'em in the ratings." He spread his arms out wide. "For crying out loud, this is the World Series for these kids—and for pretty nearly all sports fans everywhere!"

"Lazar," the man said, taking a deep breath, "how many people you really think want to see six full innings of kids playing ball?"

"Millions. We could make it five innings."

"Your boys aren't even a championship club. How do we sell your Bears to the public?"

"They're *more* than champs. They're *underdogs*. You get Cosell to do it. With a good color man. Reggie Jackson'll probably do it for you. People back home will eat it up with the right promotion. It's a natural. You people forgotten how to operate?"

The ABC man puffed up his cheeks and blew out a long breath. "Look, I'm telling you, we'll be lucky to get it on tape delay, even luckier if we could get five minutes of that tape on something like 'Wide World of Sports.' "

"What?" Marvin looked incredulous. "When McKay hears about this? You gotta be kidding. You'll be lucky if my old friend Jim doesn't come over here to do it himself, and take it away from you."

"Yeah. Lucky. Anyway, that's how I see it."

"Humph." Marvin folded his arms. "Well, I'm still talking to the other networks, so we'll see."

"Yeah, we'll see."

Most members of the two teams mingled around the field, making attempts by sign language to communicate. Tanner stood off to the side, refusing to fraternize.

Kelly, still exhausted, his eyes ringed red, stooped over the fountain to splash water on his face. A Japanese boy came over near him to sneak a smoke, concealing the cigarette in his hand. Kelly walked up to him. "I could use a taste of that," he said, pantomiming a smoke. The boy shared it with him.

Another reporter joined Marvin in the dugout, a stringer for *Sports Illustrated*. Marvin outlined the facts of the game. "See, these boys are sort of a microcosm of America. That's what they are. An honest mixture. Like this boy here . . ." Marvin put his arm around Rasula, who had been hovering near him. "This is Rasula here, a fine young man. . . ."

Rasula began buttoning Marvin's shirt, which Marvin always liked to keep unbuttoned to expose his tanned chest and gold medallion.

". . . We got some blacks, some Jewish boys. A real microcosm of our society. What are you doing, Rasula?"

"Buttoning."

"Don't." Marvin re-unbuttoned the shirt. "That's the style."

"Then how come they got more buttons than they need?"

"Bright kid, hunh?" Marvin grinned and elbowed the reporter, while pushing Rasula slightly away. "And I love their questions. Credit to America, this whole thing. Gonna be carried live on ABC's 'Wide World of Sports,' if I agree to it. I want to be careful, though, not let the kids get exploited." He patted Rasula on the head. Rasula smiled and began fiddling with the chain and medallion around Marvin's neck. "But I

guess you could say that what put this team together—what *keeps* it together"—he pushed Rasula's
hand off his neck—"is pride."

The reporter wrote "pride" in his notebook.

"What if I told you—completely off the record now
—that we got a Mexican boy on this team?" He
shoved Rasula's hands away again, and straightened
his chain. "His name is Miguel Aguilar. He's an illegal
alien and it's going to be murder to try and get him
back into the U.S. But it's worth it to give him the
chance to play in—"

"Why you wear this big old chain anyway?"

"Please, Rasula—"

"How come?"

"Style. Now please let me talk to this important
man." He turned back to the reporter. "And Miguel
wanted to come so badly that he was willing to risk
possible—"

"That ain't style, Marvin."

"—possible deportation just so he could play with
his buddies and represent America. Now, is that a
story or is that a story?"

The reporter cocked his head. "You said it was off
the record."

"Unh, well, maybe if you changed the names or
something . . ."

Shimizu, meanwhile, was in the opposing dugout,
addressing his team. "Though this is to be only an
exhibition inning," he said in Japanese, "I will not
stand for lax play. That would be disrespectful to
your opponents, and to your own country."

His team had been through many of these talks
before, and, though bored, pretended interest.

At last the inning was to be played—largely to

entice the press into greater coverage. Marvin shook hands with Shimizu, and the Japanese team took the field.

In their dugout most of the Bears were fighting just to keep awake. The change in time zones had deeply affected them. The only one ready for battle was Tanner.

Marvin hopped down into the dugout and whispered to them, "Let's not look too good, now. We want to remain underdogs." Then he took a seat next to the ABC man.

Miguel walked slowly to the plate as the lead-off batter. He stood wavering in the batter's box, asleep on his feet. The pitcher threw three quick called strikes.

Miguel remained in the batter's box, his eyes closed, while the opponents tossed the ball around the infield. The umpire touched his shoulder, waking him, signaled him "out," and directed him back to the dugout.

"*Gracias*," Miguel mumbled, trudging off.

Rudi Stein stepped up, taking a stance at the left-hander's side of the plate. He swung awkwardly at the first two pitches.

"Stein, you crud!" Tanner bellowed from the dugout. "You're not a lefty!"

"Oh, true." He walked around to the other side of the plate, and quickly swung and missed for strike three.

The closest Toby Whitewood came to getting on base was to take ball one, before striking out.

The Bears stumbled onto the field and took their positions. Or meant to. Both Ahmad and Kelly stood in right field.

"Hey," Tanner called from shortstop, "one of you guys get in center!"

"You," Kelly said.

"I can't walk that far," Ahmad groaned.

"Flip you for it."

"Never mind, I'll go. If I leave now, I should get there by noon."

Rudi Stein's first pitch went straight down into the mound. He wound up for his next pitch, trying to concentrate on not releasing it so soon, the result being that he released it too late and sent it into right field.

"Settle down, Stein," Tanner called.

Rudi gritted his teeth, and managed to send a pitch toward the plate. The batter popped it up between first and second. Neither Toby, at first, nor Miguel, at second, moved. The ball plopped between them.

Tanner raced over and picked it up. "What's the matter with you cruds!"

Some of the Japanese boys were laughing, trying to hide their giggles behind their hands.

Marvin came out to the mound. He looked around at the Bears. "Unh, you guys are doing real fine with the underdog bit, but, unh, you can go ahead and start playing now. Your arm's pretty stiff, I guess, hunh, Stein?"

"I don't feel nothin'."

"How come your eyes are closed?"

"Hunh? Oh, I only open them when I pitch."

The next batter slapped a grounder at Tanner with such force that, although Tanner reached it, it tore his glove off and carried it into the outfield.

A fly ball was hit toward Feldman in right. He drifted in and patted his glove. The ball soared over his head and bounced against the fence.

Japanese players circled the bases.

Marvin glanced nervously at the ABC man.

An easy grounder hopped toward Miguel at second. When it hit his shin, it woke him up. He looked around, confused. Again Tanner retrieved the ball, managing to hold the runner at first.

The runner took a big lead. By now Stein was reasonably awake. Suddenly he threw over to Whitewood, and they had the runner caught in a rundown between first and second. Back and forth the ball went, until Whitewood threw it into the dirt at Miguel's feet. Trying to pick it up, Miguel kicked it into center. The runner went to third. Ahmad threw in to Tillyard, covering the bag. The ball rolled through his legs. The runner came in to score.

Engelberg slammed his mask to the ground in disgust, then bellowed in pain when the mask hit his toe.

Members of the press started leaving. Marvin, watching them go, pinched his lips together and gritted his teeth.

The next batter drove one over the center-field fence for a homer.

"I'm just glad," Ahmad mumbled, "that I didn't have to move."

Now the ABC man, the last, started walking out.

"No, no, wait," Marvin begged, trotting after him.

"I guarantee you," the man said over his shoulder, "nobody back home wants to see a team get beat that bad. Not live, not on tape, not any way."

"It's just jet lag," Marvin said, catching up to him.

"I've got to get back anyway, Lazar."

Marvin grabbed his arm and turned him around. "Listen. Wait a second. Sure they stink. I know they stink. But that's what's promotable. Don't you see? They've got heart. Don't you have any sense of what sells? What happened to that old spirit that built your outfit into the sports network you are? People want to root for the underdog. . . ."

"Look, Lazar, I got to catch a plane back to the States."

"But you said—"

"I said I'd do what I could. And I will. I'll see what I can do and have somebody call you."

Marvin recognized the old brush-off. He tromped angrily back to the dugout, where the Bears were morosely returning, slinking off the field. Coach Shimizu had mercifully declared the exhibition inning over. None of the Bears spoke to one another. Tanner cried softly. Ahmad and several others sat down and stared at their feet. Engelberg leaned his face against the wall. Miguel curled up in a corner and went to sleep.

"Well," Marvin said, looking around at them and trying to keep from sinking into the same depression that gripped the team, "that's over. Buck up, Bears. That was just an exhibition. We're saving our real stuff for the game; go in as solid underdogs."

"We're solid, all right," said Ahmad, putting an arm around Rasula. "And you're lookin' at our real stuff. Looks like we got no business being here."

"Stop it!" Marvin felt panic hit him, and his face twitched. "Stop that talk!"

Nobody talked.

"There." He nodded at them. "There, there, there. Gotta do something." He charged up out of the dugout. "Phones. Gotta get to phones. Phones make everything right. . . ."

On the way home, Coach Shimizu stopped at a McDonald's to buy the team a meal. Some of the boys were talking about the fact that the Bears didn't look so hot.

He cautioned them. "I agree that their play was a bit ragged today. But I must warn you against over-confidence. They are a long way from home, and appeared tired. It is regrettable, as seems to be the case, that America did not see fit to send its very best team to face us. But then, I guess true sportsmanship has waned in the West in the last several years. It is a shame."

"What? What do you mean? Please explain, Coach," piped up some of the boys.

He waved them quiet. "I remind you that when you visit a restaurant—even"—he grimaced slightly—"such an American type as this one, the purpose is not to ask questions, but to eat."

They set to eating, dutifully.

"I must also warn you," he went on, "against further embarrassing moments like that at the airport and again this morning at breakfast. I forbid any fighting in the future, and should it occur, I will deal with the culprits severely."

"What's wrong with their coach?" a boy dared to ask.

Shimizu looked pensive. "I fear he's not actually a coach, for one thing. What he is, is a sloppy, pushy Amer— No, forgive me, I did not mean that. But I fear he does not have the purity of the sport in mind." Then, remembering himself, he added, "But I directed you to eat, not ask questions."

Marvin paced nervously, the phone glued to his ear. He had taped a thick gauze bandage over his forehead to protect it from further collisions with the low beams between the rooms. Much of his earlier confidence was gone.

Kelly, having napped and fully recovered, was now dressed spiffily in slacks and sportsjacket for a night on the town. He waved to his teammates as he strode toward the door. "Later, boys."

Marvin raised his voice a notch. ". . . The favor I'm asking is not money, Louie. I just want you to try and get this game of mine on the boards in Reno or Vegas. . . . Right. It'll be like a gag. The wire services may pick it up, once the gamblers begin taking odds. Might create some interest back home, when it hits the papers. . . ."

None of the saddened Bears seemed to be paying attention. But in truth they seldom missed much.

It was late afternoon in the now-deserted stadium where the Bears had played their disastrous inning. Almost deserted. Miguel, who had fallen asleep curled up in a corner of the dugout, not noticed by anybody, now awoke. He sat up and looked out into the vast, empty area.

His eyes slowly widened. He sprang to his feet, steadying himself against the bench. He looked around frantically, then ran out onto the field, looking for the exit.

Kelly Leak prowled the Tokyo streets, hands jammed into his blazer pockets. Cars and pedestrians packed the boulevards and sidewalks on their way home from work.

A row of motorcycles flanked a boisterous café. Kelly approached a uniquely designed bike and knelt to admire the engine. He ran his hand over the carburetor.

Suddenly a large foot clomped down on the foot-rest inches from his face. Kelly looked up. A crudely dressed biker-type, tattooed, in a tattered leather jacket and badly stained T-shirt, glared down at him.

"Nice machine," Kelly said softly.

The biker grabbed him by the hair and jerked him to his feet. Kelly clenched his fists, but saw that several other bikers had crowded around. Most of them wore white bandannas with red rising suns painted on them.

The first biker smiled and raised a clenched fist invitingly. Kelly backed off, eyeing the group. The biker spun him around and kicked him solidly in the rear, propelling him down the sidewalk.

Kelly whirled back toward him, tears of rage and frustration welling up in his eyes.

But he was helpless to go against them. He jammed his hands back in his pockets and walked away, his shoulders hunched against the derisive laughter that followed him.

FIVE

Miguel, having run back to collect his glove, found the exit and emerged into the parking area. He looked around, entirely confused and lost. All directions were the same. He looked one way, then the other, squinting against the lowering sun.

He thought he might still be dreaming, since the dream he had been having back in the dugout had to do with his being lost in a foreign place where all the people were green, with antennae on their heads.

He wished he were still dreaming. But since he was not, he knew he was truly abandoned. He grumbled some oaths in Spanish, then shrugged and walked off through the lot.

Kelly was not walking as confidently and hopefully as before. Tokyo had quickly become less exciting and more threatening. He had not supposed that there existed really tough and mean biker-types outside of Southern California—indeed, like most of the Bears, he had not imagined much at all existing outside of Southern California.

The sun was going down. Signs flickered on. He walked slowly.

Then a special vision caught his eye. He stopped. His heart seemed to stop too.

The vision was a girl, about fifteen, exiting from a Pachinko parlor.

Kelly had passed the Pachinko parlor before, and wondered what the game was. Pachinko, one of the more popular games in Japan, is something like pinball turned on end, where the balls tumble down through the gates instead of along horizontally.

But while the game had interested him before, it was only the girl he saw now. She pushed her way through the mass of pedestrians.

Kelly's unlit cigarette tumbled from his mouth. She was beautiful, with long, straight, shiny black hair.

He followed her at a discreet distance.

Marvin, through many phone calls, had watched the sun go down. Now he waited for the hotel switchboard to put through yet another call.

"Yes, hello? Operator? Could you get me . . ." His eyes popped wide. "What do you mean, no more calls? There must be some mistake. . . . Yes, yes, I'll be right down."

He hung up and trotted down to the front desk, followed by several curious Bears. He arrived breathless to see that the clerk had laid out before him on the counter two credit cards. The clerk held up a scissors.

Marvin was appalled. "You don't mean—"

"Yes, so sorry." The clerk made two quick snips across the cards.

"Did you have to cut my Diner's and BankAmericard in half?"

"Yes, so sorry. We were instructed to by the companies, Mr. Lazar. Apparently you had not only severely exceeded the limit, but were quite delinquent in payments as well."

"Well, here," Marvin said, his face flushed with embarrassment from the fact that the Bears were crowding around to witness his humiliation, "I've got others. Must have been an error in recording my last payments." He pulled out his wallet. "Take my Master Charge."

The clerk did so, with a smile, and just as quickly and neatly cut it, too, in half.

"No, no! What are you doing?"

"It appears that your Master Charge is in the same delinquent category as your others. So is American Express, so . . ." he held out his hand, smiling, "if you please."

"Heck no! No you don't!" Marvin pressed his wallet against his chest protectively.

Engelberg leaned on the counter and looked up at him. "Don't you have any cash, Marvin?"

"Cash," said the desk clerk, smiling more broadly, "would be most acceptable."

The boys peered at Marvin.

"Cash," Marvin echoed, rubbing his chin. "Cash. Who in blazes uses cash these days? I haven't seen any cash anywhere in a month."

"Cash," the clerk said, "would be most acceptable, today."

When the girl noticed Kelly trailing her, she picked up her pace. Kelly summoned his courage and trotted to catch up with her.

"Hi, there. My name's Kelly. Kelly Leak. From America. California."

She walked on, pointedly ignoring him.

"You speak any English?"

She was silent. She crossed the street. He stayed right with her, shoulder to shoulder.

"You don't, hunh? I guess that puts us in the same boat. I don't speak any Japanese."

She turned a corner, then abruptly entered a subway station. Kelly stopped for a hurried instant at a kiosk to buy an English/Japanese phrase book, then raced after her. He managed to hurtle between the doors of the train just as they were closing.

He looked around and saw her sitting a few paces away. He smiled at her.

She saw him, and sighed a discouraged sigh.

Kelly grinned as he sat down beside her. "Got a little something here to make things a little easier." He waved the phrase book, then began thumbing through it. She turned away. "*Konbanwa,*" he said hopefully, facing her. "How was that? My accent, I mean. Understand?"

She was silent.

"I'm a ballplayer, you know? You sure got beautiful hair." He flipped through the book, mumbling, "Hair, hair . . ."

Coincidentally she ran a hand down the long, black locks falling splendidly across her shoulders.

It drove him crazy. "Hair, hair . . ."

Miguel walked briskly, but aimlessly, through the labyrinth of streets among the press of pedestrians. Here and there he stopped one of the walkers and frantically tried to explain his predicament. They were as confused by, and uninterested in, his Spanish declarations and questions as were most of the Bears. And they were, of course, even less interested in him personally.

One of them, supposing he comprehended the alien yammerings, reached into his pocket and produced a few coins, which he held out to Miguel.

Miguel turned up his nose, pushed the hand away, and hurried on. He pursued a fast, meandering course here and there, looking for a landmark, any kind of recognizable building or sign that would give him a hint of where he was or where he should be headed.

What he saw, at last, was not a landmark, exactly, but it was good enough. He saw the American flag hanging outside a building. On the door was a large, round symbol indicating that this was the American Embassy—or at least the American something.

He entered the building, and went directly up to the night clerk on duty and spoke in quick Spanish—a language that, while not the native tongue even around his home, had always brought results in Southern California.

"I don't understand what you're saying," the clerk said carefully. "I . . . do . . . not . . . understand . . . what . . . you're . . . saying. Understand?"

Miguel did, in fact, understand the clerk, which was of little help. He spoke his Spanish even more quickly, desperately waving his arms for emphasis.

The clerk wrinkled his brow. "You sure you want the American Embassy?"

"*Si, si, si, si!*"

"I see. You speak Japanese?" The clerk tried some. Miguel shook his head. "French?" He tried some of that. Miguel shook his head fiercely. "Danish? Could be Danish. But I don't speak that anyway."

Miguel pounded the counter, causing the clerk to jump and incidentally sending a pad of paper and a pencil into the air. Miguel quickly grabbed the pad and pencil and began to write, laboriously:

MIGUEL AGUILAR. BAD NEWS BEARS. BASE-BALL. AMERICAN.

There were few corners of Tokyo where news about

the arrival of the Bad News Bears had not reached. One of the last places the news had reached was the American Embassy. But it had, at least, reached there.

And now the clerk reached for the phone.

Kelly stayed doggedly with the girl, even following her into the dance studio where she was taking lessons on the *koto,* at thirteen-string, guitar-like instrument.

Dressed now in a gay kimono, she strummed and sang, joined by other students and their matronly instructor.

Kelly, watching from the rear of the studio, was intrigued by the strange music performed by this angel. Almost mesmerized by her beauty, he thumbed through his phrase book, trying somehow to figure out how to put his feelings into words she could understand.

After the lesson, he trailed out after her. He moved beside her on the sidewalk. "Your singing and playing was really great. I've never met a geisha before."

He assumed that all Japanese girls who played instruments and sang sweetly and were beautiful were geishas—professional entertainers and hostesses.

She remained entirely aloof, adding to Kelly's ever-deepening frustration.

"Can't you say just a little something to me?" Even in Japanese? I mean, geishas are supposed to be real polite and stuff."

She turned and said something in Japanese—a terse and not distinctly friendly something.

"Hold it." He thumbed rapidly through his book. "Could you repeat that a little slower so I could—"

She stopped and repeated the phrase, louder and more distinctly, her hands on her hips, her lovely face thrust toward him with no hint at all of a smile. Then she spun on her heel and stalked off, even faster.

For a moment he stood looking at her. "Just my luck. A rude geisha."

Then he followed. Kelly Leak was not easily daunted, especially where matters of the heart were concerned.

Marvin filled a water glass with Scotch whiskey, took a deep swig, and sighed. Though he drank quite often, he was not ordinarily a drinker who threw them down neat like this. But times were tough.

Angry Bears stood around him.

"How could you bring us over here," Toby said, "without a dime on you?"

"Yeah, yeah," the others chimed in.

"Cash is outdated," he said weakly, taking another drink. "Whole world lives on credit."

"But you ain't even got credit," Tanner said, scowling.

"You lied to us about everything, hunh?" Rudi said.

"There was no game set up," Ahmad added, "no TV thing, no nothing!"

"Even the food stinks," Engelberg said, rubbing his belly.

"Well, blast it!" Marvin suddenly turned angry. "There would have been a game, there would have been a TV thing and all the rest, if you'd have gone to sleep last night instead of jumping around like a bunch of banshees!"

"How can we help it if their night is our day?" Ahmad asked, holding up his palms.

"You should have foreseen the problem of jet lag," Tillyard said, more calmly than the others, "and re-scheduled practice."

"Yeah," Toby said, "that's your fault."

"My fault, my fault," Marvin whined, mimicking him. "Please, fellas, give me a break and leave me alone for just a minute, hunh?"

Feldman raised his eyes soulfully toward the ceiling. "I think you're long overdue for that meeting with Jesus, Marvin."

"Jesus," Marvin repeated to himself. "How could it happen?" He paced among them, talking aloud to himself. "My big chance. Fifteen years I've been waiting for something like this, and I blow it. It was so easy. A natural." He looked at them. "Why didn't I force you guys to go to sleep last night? Everything would have been fine. Practice would have been fine. ABC would have been fine." His voice choked with anguish. "How could I screw it up?"

After a pause, Tanner said, "'Cause you stink at your job, you crud promoter."

"Back to lounge acts," Marvin moaned, "middle-aged strippers, two-bit comics. Finished as a top-line promoter."

Tillyard straightened his glasses. "How do you plan to extricate us from our present situation, Marvin?"

Marvin walked slowly through the cluster of boys, snatching his whiskey bottle en route. "Don't know. Don't know yet."

"Where you going now?" Tanner asked.

"Tub. Hot tub. Maybe get lucky and drown."

He slammed the bathroom door behind him.

They walked, sort of together, along a suburban street. Kelly's face was buried in his phrase book.

The girl, muttering angrily to herself, stopped at the door to her residence.

Kelly said something in Japanese, or in something

that approximated it. He smiled at her as she took out her key. "Well, how about it?"

Suddenly she grabbed the book from him and began looking up words in the English section.

"I said it right, didn't I?"

She traced her finger under a word. "You . . ."

"About dinner tomorrow?"

". . . miss . . ."

"What about it?"

". . . last train!" she concluded emphatically.

"Really? Well, well . . . Guess I'll have to sleep here then." He made his hands into a pillow and rested his head upon them. "I have no money for a hotel, or even a taxi." He pulled out his pockets, showing her that they were empty.

She shook her head and slapped the book back into his hands.

"Why not? I'd leave early in the morning. I wouldn't be any trouble to you or your parents, because, well . . ." the phrase came in reasonably clear Japanese, "I love you."

She giggled. Then she laughed outright. But it was not cruel. It was a warm laugh.

Kelly grinned. "Didn't think I knew that one, hunh? I was saving that for last. But I didn't think things would move so quickly between us. And it's not because"—this time his Japanese was bumbled, but perhaps understood even so—"you are beautiful."

She laughed again.

"I'm getting pretty good at this, hunh? Well, what do you say?"

She opened her door, smiling. "*Sayonara.*"

"Well, dinner tomorrow anyway," he said quickly, before she could disappear, "and no chickening out, because now that I know where you work and live I can find you and—"

She closed the door and was gone.

"Your name!" He was frantic. "I didn't even ask your *name!*"

He stood for a moment, sighed, turned, and began walking away down the street.

Her door opened. She peeked out. "Alika," she called softly.

He whirled around, just in time to see her smile and close the door again.

"Alika," he repeated as he walked. "Alika, Alika . . ."

Marvin sat in misery, soaking his body in the wooden tub. He pulled the thick bandage from his forehead and patted the red bump. It hurt. He reached down to the floor for the whiskey bottle, poured some in his glass, and gulped it down. The closed door did not keep out the voices of irate Bears.

"We've got you on fraud and child abuse, Marvin!" Engelberg cried. "Those are felonies!"

"There's still time to atone, though," came Feldman's somber tones.

"Forget about that, Feldman," Engelberg said impatiently. "We're going to sue him for every penny he's got."

"But he hasn't got anything," Toby whined.

"Then we repossess all he owns."

"By force, if necessary!" Tanner crowed.

The phone rang. Marvin heard somebody answer it. He sighed deeply and poured another drink. He heard scratching at the door, like a cat trying to get in.

"I still like you, Marvin," came Rasula's soft voice. "Marvin, that was the American Embassy on the phone. They've found Miguel. You got to go get him."

Miguel? Marvin stared bleary-eyed into his drink. He had forgotten all about the little Mexican.

"Marvin? He's been crying real hard, they said."

Slowly Marvin emptied his glass into the tub. Actually, he thought, climbing awkwardly out, it gave the bath water kind of a nice color. Maybe a marketable idea . . .

He flung a towel over his head, dressed, and left the suite, ignoring the jibes and threats some of the Bears continued to hurl at him.

He took a cab to the Embassy and, still wearing the towel over his head, went in. The night clerk quickly filled him in as much as he could, and led him over to Miguel, who was sleeping on a bench. Marvin shook him gently.

Miguel sat up with a start. His eyes were red and puffy from crying.

Marvin smiled. "Heard you had quite a tour of the city, little fella."

Tremendously relieved to see a familiar face, Miguel smiled back. He took Marvin's hand and leaned against him, yawning.

Marvin cradled him in his arms and carried him out.

Fortunately, the nasty, accusing Bears were asleep by the time they got back to the suite.

Most of them got up at a reasonable hour. Miguel and Kelly were still asleep, snoring.

"Where do you suppose Kelly was?" Toby asked.

"Who knows?" Marvin said. "Come on, you guys."

Under his supervision, the Bears were dressing. They were dressing several times over, putting shirt upon shirt, pants upon pants, socks upon socks.

"That's the ticket, guys. Tanner, you can get at least

one more shirt on top. Everybody, get as much on as you can. What you can't get on, we leave here. I want everybody ready when I get back. Then we slip by the front desk in pairs, all very casual."

The idea of beating the bill in this manner—leaving without checking out, and taking their clothes with them by simply wearing them—disturbed Feldman deeply. "The Lord is not going to like this at all," he said, tugging on his third and final pair of pants.

"We'll make it up to Him in a big way, Feldman," Marvin said, patting his head. "Don't worry. He'll be putting all the blame on me, anyway. You guys are clean."

"The blame doesn't matter," Feldman said somberly. "It's just wrong. He knows it's wrong."

"You guys are acting under orders. It'd stand up in any court."

"Are we really going back home by air freight, Marvin?" Toby asked nervously.

"Only as a last resort. And even then it'll take some doing. I'll have to work it out. But don't worry. Those cargo planes are all pressurized. They take pets that way all the time."

"We goin' like dogs and cats," Ahmad mumbled.

Tillyard looked up from his dictionary. "The Japanese word for pawnshop is *logati*, or something like that."

"And first thing you pawn, Marvin," Engelberg asserted, "is that big, ugly gold chain of yours."

"Wish it *was* gold," Marvin said, thumbing through his wallet. "But it's brass. Wonder if they might take this Sears charge card . . ."

He scooped up two handfuls of items from the top of his suitcase and held them in his palms. Included were several of the boys' watches, cuff links, key chains, and other minor valuables. "Nobody's holding out on me, right?"

"Come on, Engelberg," Ahmad said firmly, "cough it up."

"Aaaw." Reluctantly, Engelberg yielded his collapsible tin fork.

"Okay." Marvin headed for the door. "You boys sit tight. I'm going to give it one more try. Be back in an hour."

The pawnshops offered him next to nothing for the items. Marvin had decided to give up on that gambit and was returning to the hotel when he came upon a sports arena with several posters on the walls. The posters announced the upcoming rematch between heavyweight boxing champ Muhammad Ali and the famed Japanese wrestler and martial-arts expert Antonio Inoki.

Marvin chuckled at the gullibility of the public. The first match had been an utter fiasco. And the result was that now yet another match could be staged, and the public would pour in another bundle of money to see the pair in action—or non-action, if it resembled their first match.

As he passed, several people wearing ABC blazers emerged angrily from the doors.

"What's going on?" he asked a woman who was cursing to herself.

"Ali's bailed out of the match!" she said bitterly.

"Why?"

"Laryngitis."

"But that just means—"

"That he can't talk. And if Ali can't talk, there's no match."

Suddenly ideas began to whiz around his head.

His promotional mind seized upon one of them. A desperate one, to be sure. But Marvin was a desperate man.

He pushed into the exiting TV crew, elbowing savagely left and right to buck the tide and enter the arena.

In the ring in the center of the arena, wearing street clothes, Antonio Inoki, huge and dark-haired and lantern-jawed, strutted around the canvas testing the ropes and waving his big fists.

High up on the topmost tier overlooking the ring, in a makeshift booth, several dismayed and harassed officials of ABC Television screamed into phones, yelled at one another, pounded on desks, and stamped their feet.

Marvin peered in the door to the booth. It seemed to him that the mayhem inside would be nearly impossible to penetrate. Timing would be everything.

A program director clamped a phone to his ear with one hand and hurled papers around the booth with the other. ". . . But we've exhausted all legitimate replacements! So we're going vaudeville with it—a sideshow. . . . We don't have *time* to bring a name American boxer over here! Inoki's holding us to the original match time, and that's just seven hours away!"

The man jammed a cigarette into his mouth and lit it, as he listened to the phone. Then he put another cigarette in beside the first one and lit that. ". . . Darn it, we've been through all that. We had a polar bear all lined up. But it decided to hiberate. So a kangaroo was being flown in from Australia, one of those boxing types. But the sponsors pulled out because of pressure from the Society for the Prevention of Cruelty to Animals. . . ."

Another harried ABC man was on another phone.

". . . Well, if she's in Hawaii she could be here in four hours. . . . Of *course* it's absurd! It was absurd when it was *Ali* versus Inoki. Farrah Fawcett-Majors versus Inoki is no more absurd than that. So at least it's worth a try. And look, she might turn out to be a *terrific* wrestler. She already plays tennis, you know. . . . Well, at least inform her of our offer, please do that much. . . ."

A third ABC man cupped his hand over the receiver and called to the program director. "We can get a four-hundred-pound Sumo wrestler. There's one available in Yokohama."

The director slapped his desk. "Nobody back home wants to see two Japanese going at it! Use your blamed *head!*" He returned to his own phone. ". . . I *know* we're in for a million bucks already! You think I don't know what this disaster will cost us? Tell Roone we're just trying to salvage *something* out of it. . . . But we've got no more authentic options *left!* We've *got* to go the circus route!"

Marvin shook his head silently. It would be hopeless to get anybody's attention in that melee. He looked down where Inoki was pulling at the ring ropes and apparently arguing with somebody about their tension.

Marvin had to act. He had to try to talk to somebody. He squared up his shoulders, straightened his tie, put a casual and confident smile on his face, and marched into the booth.

Phone conversations boiled around him as he passed:

". . . If the SPCA isn't going to buy kangaroos, what makes you think they're going to allow two tranquilized crocodiles? . . ."

". . . But it's *fixed*, don't you understand? Nothing

can happen. Inoki's hands and one foot will be tied. Farrah would run around in a bathing suit, and he would just hop after her. . . ."

"How do you wrestle a doped-up crocodile, anyway? It would just lie there with its tongue hanging out. . . ."

". . . She could spray shaving cream or bug spray on him. . . . I don't know, we'll work out the details later. Just tell her that her career needs a shot in the arm right now. . . ."

Marvin sat down directly in front of the program director, who was still on the phone.

". . . All I know is they sent Cosell back to do a Reds-Dodgers game. We got anybody else close to Japan? . . . Who? . . . You're kidding! I don't even want to hear it!" He slammed the receiver down.

"Hi, there," Marvin said calmly. "Heard you boys were in a jam."

"Hunh? What?" The director seemed to be having trouble focusing his eyes on Marvin. "We're busy, mister. Who let you in here?" He spun around in his chair and shouted across the room. "Get Dick Button on the phone! He's supposed to be in Sapporo at some ice rink!"

"I had a replacement for you guys," Marvin said, coolly studying his fingernails, "but now I'm having seconds thoughts about it."

"What?" The director rubbed his eyes. "What did you say?"

Marvin pursed his lips and looked at the ceiling. "I'd have to clear it with the national organization, of course, which could take some doing. I'm not sure it would be worth—"

"*What* replacement?" The man leaned forward, peering at him.

"Probably wouldn't hurt, though," Marvin went on, as if to himself. "TV exposure would subject them to a lot of pressure, but it might also be a fine experience for them."

"What is it?" The man rose slowly out of his seat, his eyeballs rolling in their sockets. "What replacement? Who? When? Why? Where? Who are you?"

"Me? Oh, Marvin Lazar." He extended his hand. "Counselor. YMCA. United States of America. If you're interested, I just might have an act for you."

"An act? An *act?*" The man's eyelids fluttered out of control. "What kind of act?"

"Oh, just something I handle. It goes without saying, of course, that it is an act of proven draw in the Nielsen ratings. Otherwise I wouldn't be bothering you, would I?" Marvin smiled with half-closed eyes.

"You can get me an act?" Waves of pastel colors passed over the director's face.

"If it's worth enough to you."

Marvin got out of the taxi whistling a merry tune. He walked past the doorman into the hotel. Stepping lively to the melody, he marched past the front desk, whistling to the credit-card-destroying clerk who watched in wonderment.

He whistled up the stairs, tweeted to two kimono-clad women, and entered the suite.

The Bears stared in bewilderment at the happy whistler. They stood motionless, not only in surprise at seeing Marvin so gay, but also because they had bundled themselves into round, immobile balls of clothing. A few items of leftover apparel lay scattered on the floor. Sweat dripped from the boys' faces onto the woven mats under their bulbous feet.

Marvin stopped whistling, grinned broadly, yanked

93

a hand out of his jacket pocket to reveal a fistful of cash, and bowed low. "Gentlemen, your humble promoter has returned from a most successful expedition. Praise the free enterprise system. You can dress for summer again."

"Praise the Lord," said Feldman, sweat dripping from his nose.

All the boys quickly began tugging and scratching to pull off the layers of shirts and trousers and socks.

"Where'd you steal the money, Marvin?" Ahmad asked, eyeing him suspiciously.

"Good old American television. That's where the money is. And allow me to be the first to welcome you under your new title, the touring YMCA Junior Freestyle Wrestling Team."

"What?"

"Wrestling?"

"What do you mean?"

"I mean, boys, that we are rescued from our predicament, back on the track, ready to roll. The baseball game is just around the corner. First, there is a brief preliminary bout."

"Bout?" Rasula's voice was almost lost amid the shirts stuck over his head. "Pulmonary bout?"

"Hurry up now. Strip down and follow me!"

It was perhaps the sleaziest gym in Japan, but it was the only one available on a moment's notice for just a couple of dollars.

Marvin stood on the wrestling mat, wearing purple trunks, orange tights, and a black tank shirt. The Bears clustered around him in ill-fitting trunks, except for Kelly, who refused to participate and stood watching in street clothes.

94

"I'm just going to show you a few basic moves and how to fall," Marvin said. "First—"

"Where'd you get these duds we gotta wear?" Ahmad asked, wrinkling up his nose at his yellow trunks with holes burned in them from, apparently, cigarette ashes.

"Be glad you got them. They are, I believe, culled from the regular supply of the clientele that uses this gym. Now—"

"What do you know about this wrestling business?" Engelberg asked, trying to sketch the waistband that bit into his belly.

"What do I know? What do I *know?*" Marvin feigned annoyance. "Ever hear of Mauler Mongoose? Hunh? No? None of you? Such ignorance. Read the sports pages sometime."

"You the Mongoose?" Tanner asked, pulling up his huge trunks which kept falling to his knees.

"I was his agent. One of the all-time greats. Booked him all over the place. Really learned the business, the ins and outs, ups and downs, sidewayses and length-wises, and—"

"How we gonna learn all those wayses in one hour?" Ahmad asked.

"Just pay attention, and—" Marvin saw Kelly heading for the exit. "Hey! Where do you think *you're* going?"

"Out."

"No, no. You gotta stay. You gotta get in on this, learn some holds."

"I'm a ballplayer, not a wrestler."

"Nonsense! An athlete's an athlete. Wrestling's no different from playing ball."

"Not the way *we* play it," Engelberg muttered.

Kelly reached the door.

"Well, where you going?" Marvin called.

"Don't worry, I can take care of myself." He left.

"Hey, Marvin," Tanner said. "How much money you making off this match, you flesh-peddling crud?"

"Hardly a dime. Just enough to pay the hotel bill. You oughta be grateful for—"

"And then what?" Toby asked.

"Then?"

"Yeah, after the hotel bill, what next?"

"We take it a day at a time."

"You tell the truth about this," Engelberg asked, holding up his hand, "swear to God and hope to die?"

"Don't bring God into this," Marvin said, flexing his knees. "You'll upset Feldman."

Feldman shook his head. "The light that is Jesus is not shining down on this wrestling thing with as much warmth as it could."

"How do you know, Feldman?" Marvin smiled wryly. "Are you a wattage expert on Heavenly matters?"

"Well, if he's shining *anything* down," Ahmad said firmly, "this is one time I'm with Him, one hundred percent!"

The boys nodded.

"But what if this sucker Inoki has a mind to crack a few heads?" Ahmad went on.

The boys nodded again, looking at Marvin.

"Can't happen. It's fixed. It's a fake. Just a show."

"Who wins?" Stein asked.

"It's a tie."

"Crapola!" Tanner spat. "We go for a win, or I don't go at all!"

"We all go, Tanner, that's the deal."

"Seems like every deal you make puts us in worse shape," Ahmad said.

"No, no, we're on our way now. Couple more deals will mean we can take a regular ten-hour flight home, rather than sit for three weeks in the hull of an Iberian oil tanker."

"Oooh," Stein moaned, clutching his belly.

"But never mind all that. That's my worry. This show will go on, so the first problem's solved. Now, watch closely while I demonstrate the proper way to fall. . . ."

SIX

Antonio Inoki was in a rage, which, with somebody of that size and strength, was an awesome rage to behold. He stomped around the locker room, screaming, pounding walls and lockers, kicking over benches.

His slightly built manager trotted behind him, uttering clucking noises in an attempt to calm the powerful wrestler.

Off to the side in relative calm, stood Marvin and the program director.

"You guys can push it," Marvin said in an urgent voice. "Use a lot of ads and bulletins. You still got time for more of a buildup. Interrupt some shows with special announcements. This is a natural, I keep trying to tell you."

"You're nuts, Lazar." The director shook his head and spat on the floor. "We've lost our wallets already on this thing. Now we're just trying to cut our losses as much as we can—without investing even more in a lost cause."

Marvin snorted in disgust. "You TV people are all alike. When it comes down to it, you've really got no sense of true theater."

"What do you want from me?" The director held up his palms hopelessly. "The match is just two and a half hours away."

"The possibilities are gigantic! It's a combination of *Rocky* and *Jaws*. With a little Bowery Boys thrown in. Use your imagination! I'm talking about a show that could sweep the ratings!"

"You are talking crazy." The director shook his head, looking at Marvin out of the corner of his eye. "You are the weirdest YMCA counselor I've ever met, Lazar."

Inoki's manager left the ranting wrestler and turned to Marvin and the director. "As you can see, Antonio is most distraught," he said dolefully. "Thinks everybody insane. Worried about image, wrestling little ones. Also afraid maybe they get hurt."

"Ridiculous," Marvin said, waving off his words. "They're champions. Seasoned vets, for crying out loud."

"Bottom line for Antonio: no match."

"He can't do that!" Marvin danced frantically on one foot, then the other. "I've read his contract!" He turned to the director. "ABC will sue the pants off him, right?"

The director stared at the wall.

"Well, even if they don't sue, he's throwing away a hundred and fifty grand he would get paid. And he'll have to give back the hundred-thousand advance he already got. And the Cadillac they gave him, he'd have to give that back too."

The manager bowed and turned back to intercept Inoki and translate Marvin's words.

Inoki suddenly stopped and listened intently to the manager. He frowned. He growled. He walked over to Marvin, grabbed him by the collar, and said something harsh in Japanese.

The manager stepped up. "He say: 'Nobody touches Cadillac.'"

*　*　*

Kelly and Alika sat in a coffee shop waiting for their food. Kelly had insisted on ordering his own, picking from the phrase book. She giggled at his laborious attempt, typically hiding her mouth behind her hand.

Then Kelly cleared his throat for a question he had been waiting to ask. "Alika, do you have a boyfriend?" He repeated "boyfriend" in unsure Japanese.

They both blushed. She giggled again.

"Well, do you? Boyfriend?"

She looked at him coyly, then shook her head. She pointed at him and raised her eyebrows questioningly.

"Me? Well, a couple." He put on a cool look. "But nothing serious."

For a while they sat in awkward silence. Then she broke the ice by pantomiming a baseball swing and pointing at him.

"Yeah, right. But"—he shook his head sadly—"the game's been called off. I would have gotten you tickets, too. But I'm a ballplayer, at least, just like I told you. Good one too. Led my league in hitting the past two years. Was really looking forward to showing you my stuff in this game. But it's been, let's see . . ." He looked up the Japanese word for "canceled" and pronounced it to her.

She nodded, understanding, and lowered her eyes sadly.

"Aw, it don't matter." He fluttered his hand. "I'm getting too old for it anyway. We go home soon, fly back to California." He waggled his arms like wings. "So I guess we won't have much time together, you and me."

The food arrived. Kelly did not recognize it as being anything he had ever eaten before.

"Okay?" she asked, smiling, using the English word familiar the world over.

"Yeah, fine, perfect. Just what I ordered."

The TV lights came on, focusing on a man dressed in a tuxedo, smiling into the camera.

"Welcome, ladies and gentlemen. From the Tokyo Pavilion in Japan, I'm Dick Button, filling in for Howard Cosell this evening."

Button, many years ago a skating champion, in more recent years an ABC commentator on championship skating events, was not at all familiar with anything like what was about to take place. He did his best to appear at ease.

"We here at ABC are, um, just as upset as you all, about Muhammad Ali's unfortunate last-minute cancellation. But we do think we have a unique, extraordinary substitute match for your enjoyment."

He smiled stiffly. "We've arranged for the famed Inoki to go against a YMCA wrestling team which has lately been touring Japan. A rather unorthodox match, but bound to be exciting. Right now, let's join Antonio Inoki in the ring where he is giving a pre-match, martial-arts exhibition."

In the center of the ring, Inoki crouched in deep concentration, staring at a large block of wood. Then, with a savage grunt, he raised his hand and smashed the heel of it down, splintering the wood.

". . . As you can see," Button resumed, looking around the 12,500-seat arena, "the withdrawal of Ali has severely hurt the gate attendance."

There were, in fact, seventeen paying customers.

In the control booth, the program director winced. "Tell Button to shut up about the gate. And line up a crowd track, we're gonna need that tape for noise."

Next on the agenda, Inoki smashed a concrete block with his broad forehead.

"Isn't that marvelous, ladies and gentlemen?" Button said, rubbing his own forehead. He looked around. "Okay. The YMCA wrestling team is now entering the arena and heading for the ring."

Marvin and the Bears ran down the aisle. The boys were dressed in full baseball uniforms, waving bats and gloves in the air.

"What the devil is going on here?" demanded the program director in the booth. The staff shook their heads.

The Bears climbed up into the ring and trotted in a circle, waving to the cameras and the seventeen spectators. Inoki and his manager looked at them in disbelief.

"Hold those arms up," Marvin directed from ringside. "Keep 'em up."

Button tried to keep up a descriptive patter. "The team is garbed in, er, attractive yellow and white, actually resembling baseball uniforms. . . ."

The monitors in front of him showing the scene finally shifted back to the New York studio. Button took the opportunity to speak into his control-booth mike. "What's going on here, guys? What sport *is* this?"

"Wish I knew, Dick," came the voice of the program director back through Button's earphones. "Whatever it is, we got to keep it moving."

"Yeah, but when they called me in from Sapporo they never said anything about some crazy—"

"Just keep it moving. Hold on, they're switching back to you. . . ."

Marvin huddled with his boys in the corner. Some

102

of them glanced over at Inoki, who seemed to be arguing with his aides.

"He ain't even Japanese," Tanner said, scowling across the ring, "not with a name like Antonio."

"Why can't we at least take our hats off?" Stein whined. "We look ridiculous."

"No you don't, believe me. All part of the plan. Leave your hats on because it's best for us. Marvin's always thinking." He tapped his head. "Marvin's always on the ball."

The bell signaled the first round. Marvin hopped down from the ring apron and pushed a sheet of paper into Button's hand.

The Bears surrounded Inoki, skipping in and out.

"In order for Inoki to win the match," Button read from the paper, "he must pin all ten of the young men in one round of the three-round match. Once a boy is pinned he must leave the ring. The YMCA team can win by pinning their opponent. There is, of course, no kicking, punching, gouging . . . and, I would assume"—he glanced up toward the control booth—"no spiking."

The Bears continued to dance around, Inoki grabbing for them and missing.

In the control booth, nerves and phones jangled. "We should dump the whole thing," the director said into one of the phones. "What about last week's stock-car footage? . . . No, no, this guy Lazar didn't pay for any advertising. I never even heard of him until today. . . . What do you mean, *there's no YMCA wrestling team in Japan?*"

Inoki stabbed for the darting boys. He managed to brush a couple of them and spin them around. Rasula, giddy with excitement, scooted around the six-foot-four wrestler doing an Ali shuffle.

103

"Think you're bad, hunh, sucker? You ain't bad as *us!*"

Rasula threw a few jabs. Inoki grabbed him and flipped him over, trying to do it gently. But Rasula flopped to the mat hard.

Ahmad charged angrily, punching Inoki stiffly in the stomach. Inoki grunted, reached him, and sent him thudding to the mat on his rear.

Inoki kept whispering to the boys and to his corner.

"Inoki wants you cool it," came the whispered translation from Inoki's manager.

But the Bears didn't cool it. They clambered aboard him from all directions, catching his face with knees and elbows as he tried to shake them off without hurting anybody.

Tillyard accidentally kneed Inoki in the nose. Inoki howled in pain. Ahmad stuck a finger in his eye. Pulling Ahmad's hand away, Inoki unfortunately hit Tanner in the jaw.

Tanner reeled backwards, then recovered and dove for Inoki's ankle—teeth first. He bit down hard. Inoki bellowed and kicked up his legs, sending Bears flying.

". . . Fine move by Inoki," Button announced, "good leg action . . ."

Inoki put one hand over his bloodshot eye and held his ankle with the other, hobbling around the ring while he yelled at the referee.

The bell ended the round.

"Let's go to a commercial, Dick," the director said into his mike.

"Let's go to a bar," Button said.

Inoki, in his corner, was furious. His aides kept patting him here and there to try to calm him down.

Marvin was trying to calm down the Bears.

"I thought this was supposed to be an exhibition," Engelberg moaned, rubbing his bruised stomach.

"Well, don't be so rough! What'd you bite him for, Tanner?"

"Got hungry," Tanner muttered, rubbing the welt on his chin.

"Don't get sassy with me."

"Well, he almost broke my *jaw!*"

"And did you see what he did to Little Bro?" Ahmad asked, his eyes flashing.

"Sucker's gonna get *his* this round," Rasula said.

"Think you better count me out of this next round," Tillyard said, sniffing. "Asthma's kicking up."

"Okay, guys," Marvin put his arms around them, "everything's okay now. Don't lose your cool. Just relax and don't fight back. He knows the game. He'll make it easy for you."

But Inoki had informed his aides that he wanted no more of this nonsense. He wanted to end it and get out to his Cadillac.

At the sound of the bell he raced out into the ring, grabbed Tanner, and pinned him to the mat. The ref motioned Tanner out of the ring. Then Inoki grabbed Tillyard, who was already trying to escape between the ropes, dragged him back in, and pinned him—despite the valiant efforts of Ahmad, Rasula, and Engelberg to assist their comrade.

". . . Inoki seems to be asserting himself at this point . . ." Button carried on.

"He's going berserk!" Toby yelled to Marvin.

"What about the *tie?*" Ahmad cried, trying to avoid Inoki's lunges.

Inoki latched onto the squirming Rudi Stein and

tried to pin him, while several other Bears hung onto the wrestler's back. Engelberg pulled down Inoki's trunks.

Inoki released Stein in order to hoist his pants.

Tanner, ignoring the rules, reentered the ring and set immediately to gnawing again on Inoki's ankle. Inoki flipped him over and pinned him again.

Rasula jumped down from the ring, pulled some baseballs out of the duffel bag, and began pelting Inoki with them.

Inoki looked around wildly for the source of the clobbering.

Now, in the booth, the ABC crew was becoming interested in the match. Some of them even shouted encouragement.

Inoki, ignoring the thudding baseballs for a moment, pinned Toby and Feldman at the same time, one under each arm. Then he similarly pinned Ahmad and Miguel.

Tanner, already twice ejected from the ring by the ref, couldn't stand the idea of approaching defeat, and climbed back in. He took a flying leap at Inoki's rear and kicked him across the ring. Inoki slammed into the ropes and rebounded to the center of the ring where he landed, dazed on his back.

The Bears were on him like army ants, holding him at every possible point. The referee counted him out.

Then, while Inoki dizzily rubbed his nose and rear, the victorious Bears ran around the ring, yelping and hopping and cheering.

". . . Perhaps we have not heard the last of this YMCA team," Button said, smiling into the camera.

In the control booth, the director said into the phone, "Well, if they aren't touring Japan, they *oughta* bel Some of you New York boys see if you can get a line on them. . . ."

Marvin started across the ring to give his condolences, but one look at Inoki's rage-contorted face caused him to back away. "Some other time then . . ."

He raced off to join the jubilant Bears heading for the exit.

The Japanese countryside whooshed by outside the windows of the splendid, 135-mile-per-hour "Bullet Train."

The Bears and the Japanese baseball team were in the dining car, heads pushed together to scan an article in the new issue of *Sports Illustrated*. Under a photo of Tanner taking his flying kick at Inoki's backside, the headline read: THE DIM FUTURE OF SPORT.

Gradually they scattered into small groups. Four of the Japanese boys concentrated diligently on their schoolwork.

"How come you guys are always studying?" Tanner asked them. "I mean, don't you guys know it's summer?"

They smiled politely and continued their work.

At another table, Ahmad, Rasula, and Tillyard watched a Japanese boy who was demonstrating a particular batting stance for the Americans. He cocked the imaginary bat and lifted his front leg off the ground in the style of the great Japanese home-run hitter.

Ahmad scratched his head. "Sadaharu who?"

"Oh," Tillyard said. "Sadaharu Oh."

"Oh," Ahmad said, not really understanding.

At the expression of the name, the Japanese boys nodded reverently.

"Well, if that's his batting stance," Ahmad said, hooking a thumb at the demonstrator's raised leg, "he can't be all that good. 'Sposed to keep those legs planted till the pitch is on its way."

"He's hit more homers than Ruth," continued Tillyard, the statistics expert. "And he'll be passing Henry Aaron's record soon."

"Really?" Ahmad was disappointed to hear, from so reliable a source, that his hero was soon to be surpassed.

Nearby, the pitcher for the Japanese team was demonstrating for Rudi Stein the various proper grips on the ball for various pitches. Rudi watched attentively.

Feldman leaned over a table to draw a picture of a cross on a napkin. The Japanese boys studied it. "He died for our sins," Feldman said.

At a table at the end of the dining car, Marvin, dressed in a shiny new dark-blue suit, talked with an interpreter and Coach Shimizu. "People just fell in love with us." Marvin smiled broadly, in a very good mood. "Just fell plumb in love." He lit a cigar while the translator passed on his words to Shimizu. "That's why they're broadcasting the game. A friend of mine is even taking bets in Vegas on the outcome."

Shimizu nodded at the translation, then spoke. Translated, he said, "We are certainly not going to do anything as ridiculous as your wrestling match." He smiled slightly.

So did Marvin. "You don't have to go that far, Shmito. But we've *got* to get people in your country as interested in this thing as our people are. This picture-taking tour we're going on is peanuts compared to what we should be doing." He held up a copy of the *Sports Illustrated* article. "We've got to have a Japanese version of this!"

He slapped the magazine proudly down in front of Shimizu. Toby and Engelberg took seats at the table with them.

Shimizu spoke. "It is my understanding that the article is about fraud in sports," the translator said for him.

"It doesn't matter," Marvin said. "It's a cover story in a big national publication."

"Didn't you read what they said about you, Marvin?" Toby asked.

"Big deal. I don't—"

". . . 'Self-styled promoter Marvin Lazar,'" Engelberg read from the piece, "'oozes with more oil than the entire reserves of Arabia. . . .'"

Marvin waved it off. "They got to toss in some dirt to make things interesting. That's what's wrong with journalism today. But it doesn't really matter, from our point of view. The main thing is to get people talking about you. Take a look at that photo, hunh? That'll get 'em talking. . . ."

In time the car became quiet, as the boys settled down for the ride.

Marvin strode through the car, looking around. "Where's Kelly? Anybody seen him?"

"He didn't come," Tanner said.

"What do you mean, he didn't come?"

"He didn't get on the train."

"He's not here at all?" Marvin frowned. "Little goldbricker missed a good chance to get his picture in the papers."

People were packed like sardines inside the Pachinko parlor, watching the steel balls dropping through the vertical machines. Players sat like zombies following the course of action.

Alika was cashier. She stood behind the counter, busily dispensing boxes of balls.

"*Konechiwa!*" Kelly smiled proudly at his greeting.

She smiled briefly in surprise, but as quickly the smile vanished.

Kelly swung an imaginary bat. "The game's back on. The rest of them went off somewhere on some publicity thing."

Alika glanced uneasily down the counter toward her father, a small, wiry, somber-looking man.

Kelly followed her glance. "I know you said not to come by when you're working at your dad's place. But I'd just like to meet him, you know?"

Her father frowned over at Kelly. Alika tried discreetly to motion Kelly to the door.

But he stayed where he was. "I won't bug you. I'll just play one of these games and then we'll go eat." He pantomimed eating. "Lunch."

He handed her some money. She refused it, shaking her head.

"What's wrong? Isn't that the price of a game?"

Her father came up.

"Hi. I'm Kelly."

The father pointed at a sign overhead, in Japanese symbols, then pointed at the door.

"I don't get it. What'd I do wrong?" He held up his money and scratched his head.

Alika, too, pointed at the sign, and shook her head again.

Her father walked over to two employees, spoke to them, and directed their attention to Kelly.

Alika grabbed Kelly's arm and urgently turned him toward the door.

"Okay, okay, I can take a hint. Geez." He walked out.

The teams of boys debarked in Kyoto, the ancient historic capital of Japan. They were led over to line up in front of an old shrine, and instructed to hold up large plaques indicating "TEAM JAPAN" and "TEAM AMERICA."

Three photographers snapped pictures.

Then they boarded two vans that took them to the Kiyomizu Temple, high on a hill overlooking Kyoto. Marvin staged another shot, having the Japanese pitcher pose in mid windup while Engelberg took a hitter's stance with a bat. Photographers recorded the scene from all angles, as directed by Marvin.

Then they went to a huge statue of Buddha, at fifty-three feet tall the largest bronze statue in existence. The two teams lined up in rows behind it. One boy from each team held up his country's flag.

Shimizu watched all this picture-taking and posing with deepening disapproval. It was, in the view of some Japanese like him, rather sacrilegious.

Finally they left the shrines and moved down into Kyoto itself. The group walked along a pleasant street, Marvin conversing one-sidedly with an impassive Shimizu. The interpreter never missed a word.

". . . One thing to do is to build up a little animosity between the two teams. It's a must. Done all the time. A few nasty things in print and so forth. Like at the airport, and at breakfast, when the two boys went at it—that sort of thing. Excellent. That's one thing we're good at in the U.S. We practically invented publicity. . . ."

A militaristic motorcade passed slowly by, Jeeps

carrying members of a right-wing political group. A loudspeaker blared out an emotional national tune.

Shimizu stopped and listened, his eyes revealing respect and a sort of longing.

Marvin was frustrated by Shimizu's inattention to the conversation. "Look, Shmee, you got to give me some input here. I mean, we only got one week to put this thing together. I mean, you got to come up with some ideas from your side. I'm always receptive to ideas. So you got to help move these plans along."

Shimizu ignored him, his attention riveted on the motorcade and music and patriots who waved from the Jeeps.

Engelberg tugged at Marvin's arm. "Is this interpreter's salary coming out of our percentage, by any chance?"

"Why?"

"'Cause he's only translating what *you* say. Their coach ain't saying nothing. That's only worth half as much."

"Don't worry about it, Engelberg." Marvin gently removed Engelberg's fingers from his sleeve. "You're going to be a rich man." He turned back to Shimizu. "Now listen, Shmoozu—"

The interpreter abruptly stopped him with a warning look, finger over his lips. "This is a solemn moment for Mr. Shimizu," he whispered.

Marvin sighed and waited for the last of the Jeeps to disappear.

They wandered further through a beautiful landscaped garden.

". . . Promos, commercials, endorsements of every kind," Marvin continued his message to Shimizu. "We've got to cover all possible angles. TV is the most important. TV is where the money—"

Shimizu interrupted. Translated: "Why all this for a children's game, Mr. Lazar?"

"Think of what this will do for Japanese baseball," Marvin responded.

Shimizu stopped walking and regarded Marvin with a mysterious smile. He spoke. Translated: "How much money do you stand to make out of this charade, Mr. Lazar?"

"Charade?" Marvin blinked slowly, then smiled back. "Hopefully a bundle. I know you think I'm a jerk, Coach. And you've got good cause, I guess. Maybe a lot of people feel that way about me." He paused and looked off. "But a chance like this doesn't come along too often. And I don't get many chances anyway. So I don't want to blow it. And all this whole thing can be darned good for you too. Buy a lot of equipment for your boys. Make you a little money for yourself, even. We don't have to like each other to work with each other."

Shimizu smiled more warmly. Suddenly he spoke in clear English. "I still get rights to Sweden?"

Marvin stepped back, stunned, then laughed and threw his arm around Shimizu's shoulder. "So I underestimated you. Been doing that all my life. You really made a sap out of me."

Shimizu bowed slightly, smiling.

They sat down on a bench.

"So now," Marvin said, squaring his shoulders, "what's the top-rated show in Japan?"

" 'Columbo.' "

"No, no, I mean talk show. Like we got Carson, 'Good Morning, America,' and so forth."

They watched the boys crossing a serene pond, hopping from rock to rock. Tanner was playfully pushed

113

into the shallow water by the boy with whom he had fought earlier. Everybody laughed.

Shimizu lapsed back into Japanese, speaking to the interpreter. The translator passed it on to Marvin.

Marvin wrinkled his brow. " 'The All-Star Family Singing Hour'? What kind of game show is it?"

"Several celebrities bring on their nonprofessional families or friends, and sing," the translator explained, without waiting for Shimizu to speak. "At the end, the judge decides who wins."

Marvin's eyes widened. "Prime time, hunh?"

Shimizu nodded, then spoke again in Japanese. "But it is impossible. You must be a celebrity to enter. On the other hand, there is a rather popular afternoon show—"

"What do you mean, impossible! You *are* a celebrity!"

Shimizu raised his eyebrows.

"You're the coach of the best team in the Far East. A source of national pride. Developing the youth of the Orient! You're a goshdarned *giant!*"

Shimizu waved his hand humbly.

"You are!" Marvin stood up and paced back and forth in front of him. "Big as Vince Lombardi was in our country, or even Knute Rockne, for Pete's sake. More important in your own country, in the long run, than Sadaharu Oh! I'm gonna prove it to you. We're gonna do that show. *You* are. You and your boys are gonna sing on prime-time TV!"

Shimizu closed his eyes. "Oh my," he said in soft English.

Marvin discovered that one of the show's producers had studied at UCLA, and applied on him some clever salesmanship, including some rather misleading, if

114

not downright dishonest, suggestions that Coach Shimizu just might be suffering from a rare terminal disease and that the show should not miss its chance to have him on.

The producer agreed that he wouldn't want to miss such a chance, asked how things were lately in Southern California, including the women on the beaches, and slated Shimizu and his team for the show.

And so now they all waited in the wings as the Japanese master of ceremonies pranced out onto the stage in front of the audience and rattled off a rapid sing-song monologue as slick and sharp as any in the U.S.

Shimizu paced nervously backstage, grumbling to himself. Behind him his team, in uniform, huddled in fright.

Marvin attempted to comfort him. "Don't worry, Schitzu, these shows are a piece of cake. They're all nonprofessionals, just like yourself, don't forget."

Shimizu tried to hum. Only a squeak came out. He cleared his throat and tried again. The squeak was joined by a gargle. He swore a Japanese oath.

Marvin patted his back. "I heard you in practice, and you're great. Once you get in front of that audience, bathed in the spotlight"—Shimizu winced and shivered—"you'll knock 'em dead."

The first group was introduced on stage. It was a well-known comedian and his family and in-laws. The comedian broke up the audience with his quips. Then the orchestra struck up, and the family sang a beautiful old Japanese folk song. They were very good.

Backstage, Marvin paced among the frightened Far Eastern Champs, patting them on their heads. "They call that singing? That was nothing compared to what you can do. You're going to win this thing."

The next group sang. It was a lovely family with seven children. After one chorus of a pop song, the adults stopped, and the kids took over. They launched into a tight, neat, and precise upbeat rock number.

The judges smiled their approval.

Backstage, the boys were numb. One tried to leave, but Marvin stopped him. Another sank to the floor, and Marvin had to hoist him up under the arms.

Shimizu and the boys were called out onto the stage.

They walked out uncertainly, huddled in a tight group. The audience applauded politely. The host asked Shimizu a couple of questions, and was greeted with silence. Shimizu stood staring, stiff as a board.

The boys were asked to introduce themselves, and they responded so weakly that they couldn't be heard.

Marvin was grateful that the host signaled for a commercial. He trotted out onto the stage, dragging the interpreter with him. "Lighten up, Shee. You're going to dazzle 'em." He patted each of the boys on the cheeks.

The commercial was ending, and the host and producer tried to push Marvin off the stage.

Marvin pushed the interpreter toward them. "Tell the jerkos to go easy on this bunch. Can't he see they're nervous? Who's he think Shizitzu is, Bob Hope? He can't trade jokes. He's a national treasure! And they shouldn't have to follow some pro group like those blamed Japanese Jackson Five either!"

Finally the Bears rushed out and pulled Marvin off the stage.

The host gave the signal to start, and Shimizu and his boys stumbled through a discordant version of

"Do, Re, Me," from *The Sound of Music*. They forgot most of the lyrics and much of the melody and a good bit of the rhythm. The orchestra got mixed up trying to follow them.

Just before finishing the song, the boys began bowing ferociously. And with the mercifully concluding notes from the frazzled orchestra, they ran pell-mell off the stage.

They ran past Marvin and never stopped running until they were out of the building.

Marvin watched them go. "Well, that oughta get people talking," he said to his sympathetic Bears.

High atop the bleachers overlooking a complex of baseball fields and spectator stands stood Marvin and Shimizu, along with an ABC man and the interpreter. Shimizu, unable to shake the effects of the debacle at the TV show the night before, sagged and moped with depression. The ABC man, bored, shifted uneasily from one foot to the other.

Only Marvin was upbeat about matters, his mind racing a mile a minute. He felt truly in his element, now that he was engaged in the actual act of promoting, sorting out details, making decisions. Like most promoters and public relations men, he felt best when he was on the attack, especially since so much of the time he was on the defensive trying to patch up mistakes.

He pointed to the nearest diamond. "How about this one?"

"Ten thousand," Shimizu said in weary Japanese.

Marvin put an arm around him. "Cheer up. You know what the ratings were last night? Dynamite! You'll probably get a series. Okay." He pointed to another park. "How about that one?"

"Twenty-two thousand seats," Shimizu said, through the interpreter.

Marvin frowned thoughtfully. Then he waved toward the huge, bowl-like stadium farthest from them on the opposite side of the complex. "What's that mamoo over there seat?"

"The Yomiuri Giants play there. It's a major-league park. Forget it."

"What's it seat?"

"Fifty-five thousand, but—"

"See if it's free on the eighteenth," Marvin said, cutting off the interpreter. He turned to the ABC man, who was scuffing his toe idly. "That's the one, all right. You guys get behind this, check it out."

"Stop it, Lazar," the man said grumpily. "Promotion-wise, you don't have the time. You could never get enough of a campaign cranked up. You'd never get close to filling that thing."

"Oh I won't, hunh?" Marvin took him by the lapel, which seemed to cause the man great discomfort. "You just get your own end of things cranked up. You ain't even seen me in action yet. You saw the wrestling match? The TV show? Peanuts. Did that with the little finger of my left hand. You guys are so used to being little cogs in your darned corporate machinery that you've forgotten what one man can do when he sets his skills and talent and experience and will to it."

"I saw seventeen people at the wrestling match."

"Oh yeah? That's because it was *your* show. I just came in at the last second to bail you out. This show's *mine*. My talent, my plan. You come aboard, and I'll put ABC back on the map, along with Japan."

Shimizu turned and glared at him.

Marvin took his elbow and leaned close to his ear. "Leave it to American know-how, Shoo."

Marvin was as good as his word, which is to say that selling kids on the commercial market was not beyond his range of capabilities. Using his knowledge of the desperate corporate warfare in the cereal market, he quickly lined up a commercial.

The TV studio was a serious place, the American crew, working in unfamiliar surroundings with unfamiliar subjects, continually mopping sweat from their brows.

"Okay," said the man with the clapboard, "Wheaties commercial take three." He clapped the board's sections together and backed out of camera range.

The camera focused on Kelly Leak, seated at a long table, a bowl of Wheaties in front of him.

"And how long," said the announcer, "have the scrappy San Fernando Valley Bears been eating Wheaties?"

"Since I was four," Kelly said.

The camera panned down the table, stopping at the face of each Bear in turn, all with spoons poised over heaped bowls.

"Since I was five," Stein said.

"Since I was two," Toby said.

"Since I was six," Engelberg said. As the camera shifted along to Tanner, Engelberg added, "But I been eating Cheerios and Applejacks for just about as long. Sometimes mix 'em all together, and add—"

"Cut!" The director stalked angrily up to the table. "This is a Wheaties commercial, kid!"

"Well, you don't want him to lie, do you?" Feldman asked.

"Get this straight, kiddos," the director snarled. "We're paying good money for—"

"You didn't say we were getting paid, Marvin," Tanner said.

"Didn't want to bore you with the details."

"How much?"

"Usual percentage."

"Then I'm declaring myself a free agent," Tanner said huffily, crossing his arms. "Gonna negotiate my own contract."

The director threw up his arms.

"Easy, easy," Marvin said, patting him on the back. "Just remember, boys, the Japanese kids are doing their part too."

"Well, what's this got to do with our *game?*" Engelberg asked, chewing a mouthful of Wheaties.

"It'll get people talking about you. Okay, come on. Everybody get their spoons ready and look at the camera."

The director sighed. "Ready with take four."

Another commercial that played over Japanese television showed the monster gorilla Godzilla storming through Tokyo, smashing buildings below him, roaring, and belching smoke. Then into the scene strode a member of the Far Eastern champs, wearing his Team Japan uniform and carrying a bat over his shoulder.

The monster stopped in his tracks, eyeing the small boy at his feet.

Then the boy hauled off and, with a mighty swing of the bat, slammed Godzilla in the shins. Godzilla howled in pain and slumped to the ground.

The camera zoomed in on the boy, who put his foot on top of the gorilla's carcass and held out the bat. The camera zoomed in closer on the bat itself, then on its trademark, as the announcer praised the superior quality of this manufacturer's product.

Coach Shimizu, watching the commercial in his living room, closed his eyes and shook his head.

Marvin left no stone unturned. To Shimizu's team practice the next day, Marvin brought the Bears and several reporters, including an ABC-TV crew.

As the Far Eastern champs went through infield practice, reporters gathered around Shimizu.

He was becoming more comfortable with reporters, or at least more resigned to their presence, and he answered all questions with good nature. One of the reporters, smiling, asked him if he really knew the words to the song they tried to sing on TV recently. Shimizu puffed up his chest and delivered the first verse. They all laughed, though Shimizu's face was red.

The coach stepped away from them and yelled some instructions out to his team. As usual they were drilling very hard, sweating with effort.

In the Bears' dugout, the ABC man, recording some interviews to be used on game day, held up a mike between himself and Ahmad.

"You boys aren't given much chance to win. Think that'll bother you, cramp your style of play, destroy your confidence?"

"Naw. We ain't much for style anyway. We'll hold our own. We got the fact of underdogs going for us."

The announcer moved over to Tanner. "It's widely assumed that the Bears are overmatched in this contest. Do you think that will—"

"I'm sick and tired of hearing how we're overmatched!" Tanner shouted, kicking the water cooler. "You guys don't know nothin' except boxing and ice-

121

skating. You phoney baloneys just wait! We'll show you a thing or two about the national pastime that made our country great!"

The announcer nodded and turned to the cameraman. "It'll be all right when we cut it and put it together."

He moved over to Marvin. "Mr. Lazar, how do you feel about the upcoming game?"

"Aw, they're probably ten times as good as the Bears are, technically," Marvin said, giving the camera his sincere look. "That is, on paper, the Japanese boys have got it over us at every position. And they've got depth. And of course they've got the homefield advantage. But we aren't playing the game on paper"— he smiled cockily—"and these boys of ours have *heart*. They're fighters. They have that special quality. I think a lot of people will be surprised."

"We understand, Mr. Lazar, that a lot of people back home are already surprised by some of the things they've seen and heard about the activities over here so far."

Marvin chuckled. "Yes, I can imagine so. Interesting, the ideas these boys come up with. . . ."

Once the interviews were wrapped up, the TV crew headed for the press booths overlooking the large stadium, where technicians were making preliminary preparations for coverage of the upcoming game. Marvin followed.

Kelly, sitting in the stands not far away, watched them with little interest. Feeling moody and depressed, he shunned all further publicity, and even refused to hang around with the team.

In the outfield bullpen, Rudi Stein was getting pitching instructions from an unlikely source: his opposing pitcher, the boy who had given him some pointers earlier. Now the boy was advancing the instruction, patiently demonstrating his special submarine delivery, firing dropballs to his catcher.

Stein then copied his moves, improving on each pitch. Everything was done without verbal communication. Through sign language and smiles and nods, the language barrier was overcome.

The Japanese pitcher corrected Stein's grip on the ball slightly, and Stein fired another pitch.

The Japanese catcher felt it smack into his mitt. He dropped the ball and mitt and rubbed his hand in mock pain.

The pitcher pounded Stein on the back in congratulations, while a photographer snapped the happy picture.

In the press booth, Marvin was on the phone, looking down upon Shimizu's team at practice.

". . . So what are the odds in Reno, Louie? . . . Already twenty-to-one underdogs?" He guffawed. "Super! I love it! Is there a lot of action? . . . Bettors actually lining up? Terrific! Super! . . . Well, I know the effort you're putting into it, Louie, and I can't thank you enough. . . . Of course, friend, I'll think of a way to thank you. Putting it on the boards really gave us a shot in the arm. . . ."

His mood suddenly changed as he happened to glance out toward the bullpen. ". . . Right. Unh, I got to go, Louie. . . . Yeah, I know, I know what I'm already into you for . . . Right. Gotta run. Bye."

He grabbed Shimizu and headed toward the bullpen.

They marched up to Stein and the opposing pitcher and catcher, glowering.

Shimizu called his pitcher and catcher to him and set to ranting his disapproval.

Marvin elbowed the photographer aside, grabbed Stein's elbow, and walked him out of earshot. "What in blazes are you doing, Stein? You switched sides or something?"

Stein wrinkled up his nose and cocked his head quizzically. "Why? I've just been practicing. I learned this really neat submarine pitch. Wanna see it? My control is really getting good now."

"*No*, I don't wanna see it!" He glanced over his shoulder at the waiting photographer and pulled Stein closer. "Listen, you ever heard of two opposing pitchers helping each other out with new pitches before a World Series game? Hunh?"

"Well, no, but we were just—"

"How do you think it looks? People'll think this is a picnic. You're not supposed to be taking your underdog label lightly, Stein. You're supposed to be mad about it and come out fighting. And here I see you smiling like a baboon for some photographer, practically sitting in the enemy's lap! We want people to care who wins this game!"

"We care about winning; it's just that—"

"Then care a little about sharing your secrets with your opposition, for Pete's sake!"

"I didn't show him nothing, Marvin, honest."

Marvin took him by the shoulders and narrowed his eyes. "Didn't you show him how you gripped the ball?"

"Yeah, but—"

"Don't you think he's getting the book on what you can and can't do?"

"Yeah, but—"

124

"Yeah, but what?"

"Yeah, but I couldn't do *nothing* until he showed me how!"

Marvin rolled his eyes in frustration.

SEVEN

Alika walked past the front desk at the hotel and went on to a far corner of the lobby, where she took a seat primly on the bench.

Shortly, Marvin and the Bears marched somberly into the lobby and headed for the elevator.

Kelly trailed morosely behind them. He heard his name called, and stopped. He turned slowly around and saw Alika sitting on the bench, smiling at him.

"Kelly," she repeated in her wonderful accent.

He almost smiled, but didn't. He ambled over and took a seat a bit away from her on the bench and nodded hello. He was wary, having not forgotten the unpleasant ejection he received from the Pachinko parlor.

She reached down beside her and picked up a basket and put it on her lap. She handed him a piece of paper, a note.

He took it cautiously, opened it, and read the large and careful printing:

"Kelly. Big mistake. So sorry I and father rude to yoo. Must be 18 years old to play in Pachinko. It is law. Sign in Pachinko says law. Please forgive."

Kelly brightened and looked at her. "The law? Why didn't you just say so? You know I couldn't read the blamed sign."

She looked down at her hands folded on top of the basket.

"So that's it," he said, looking a little glum. "I don't look eighteen, hunh? Funny. I thought I looked close to twenty. Lot of girls think I'm—" He stopped, seeing her flush red. He pointed to the basket. "What's that?"

She continued to blush. "Piks . . . piks . . . piksniks lunch!" She beamed at him.

"Gee . . ."

Marvin had gone out. The Bears lounged around the suite in various poses of idleness. Several of them stood by the window overlooking the ragged park below, where a bunch of small girls were playing softball.

"Looka them," Engelberg said. "They can really fire that thing around."

"Softball's for sissies," Tanner scoffed, "and girls. Anybody can catch and hit that punkin."

"I beg to differ," Tillyard said, raising an index finger. "Softball is one of the fastest and most demanding sports. The pitcher is much closer to the batters. Basepaths are significantly shorter. The game requires—"

"Even *you* could hit that thing," Tanner said.

"Hmm."

Marvin burst jubilantly through the door, balancing a tower of boxes on his arms. "Okay, guys, give a look!"

He dumped the boxes on the floor, knelt beside them, and began opening them up. They contained bright, brand-new yellow-and-white uniforms. "RCA" was printed in large lettering across the lower backs of the shirts. Above that were the numbers, and above the numbers were stenciled the boys' last names.

"Christmas has come a little early," Marvin said, tossing the uniforms out to the boys. "Look at these, will you? Beautiful! Custom-made! Professional! The whole bit!"

The boys held up the uniforms in front of them, taken by surprise, and confused.

"But we already got uniforms," Toby said. "We got our own uniforms we always wear."

"Not like these," Marvin said, a trace of irritation in his voice. "Rags is what you got. Notice I insisted on the same color combination. In the *majors* they don't get uniforms better than these."

Ahmad examined his new garment apprehensively. "I usually wear number forty-four," he said.

"What?"

"Forty-four. That's Hank Aaron's number."

Marvin walked over and stooped beside him. "Sorry, old buddy. I meant to make it the same numbers. But look here." He took the shirt from Ahmad and held it up. "Your name's written out. Isn't that nice?"

Ahmad didn't reply.

"And you're number eight. That's Joe Morgan, all-star second-baseman on the Reds. Two-time most valuable player. And he's, um, like Aaron, in some ways."

"He's black, you mean. That's all. He don't hit all them home runs."

"Well, Aaron's retired anyway." He patted Ahmad on the head. "You want to be up-to-date, don't you?"

"Where's the third?" Tillyard turned his shirt over and over, searching it.

"What?"

"It's got 'E.R.W. Tillyard' on it, but no 'Third.' "

"There wasn't room for all that garbage, Tillyard.

You guys don't have backs as broad as Wilt Chamberlain's, you know."

Tillyard looked at the shirt, his eyes lowered. "Chico was sure good to us."

"Chico?"

"Yeah. Back in California. He gave us our regular uniforms."

"Well, Chico's not paying us thirty thousand dollars to wear his insignia like RCA is."

The doorbell rang. Marvin went to answer it.

"What's four percent of thirty thousand, Tillyard?" Engelberg asked.

"Twelve hundred," Tillyard said quickly.

"Darn right," Marvin said, opening the door. "Think of those college educations."

Several members of the Japanese team stood at the door. They nodded hello and took off their shoes.

"What, unh, what's going on?" Marvin scratched his head.

Several Bears came over to the door.

"Some of us are going to the game with them," Feldman said. "Pro game tonight."

"What?" A frown crossed Marvin's face as he looked back and forth from one group to the other. "Tonight you guys were going to the movies."

"They invited us to the game," Toby said.

"How could they invite you? They can't even speak English."

"We understood them."

"Unh, excuse us for a minute, gentlemen." Marvin closed the door on the Japanese boys and turned to the Bears. "I wish you guys would get this through your heads: You shouldn't fraternize with the enemy this close to your own game."

"That's what *I* say," Tanner muttered.

"The Lord moves in strange and wondrous ways," Feldman said earnestly. "And He's guiding us into a wholesome friendship with our brothers in this foreign clime."

Marvin chuckled in spite of himself. "Easy for *Him* to say. He doesn't have a percentage of the gate."

"We just want to see this Saddle Harry dude," Ahmad said.

"That's Sadaharu Oh," Tillyard corrected.

"Whatever. The dude they been saying is so good."

Marvin thought for a moment. Noting that the Bears seemed quite committed to going and not wanting to risk a scene with them, he said, "All right, but keep a low profile."

"What's that mean?" Ahmad asked.

"That means, don't let a photographer within a mile of you."

The boys started to file out.

"I'm staying here with you, Marvin," Rasula said.

Marvin was already thinking about plans of his own. "No, you go along, Rasula. I've got an appointment."

"I'll go with you."

"You can't. It's a private appointment."

Rasula went over to the corner to pout as the boys left.

Most of the Bears had never been to a professional baseball game, even in California. The size of the crowd and the drama of the game being played under the lights awed them.

The contest was a tight, 2–2 pitchers' duel until the bottom of the seventh. The great Japanese hitter took his place at the plate. On the back of his shirt was the name "OH" and the number "1."

As he awaited the pitch, Sadaharu Oh cocked his front leg off the ground. He swung at the first pitch—a smooth and classic swing—and the crack of the bat on the ball echoed in the stadium.

Fifty-five thousand fans rose to their feet to watch the ball sail out of the park.

The Bears were among those who had risen.

The cheering rose to a deafening roar as the mighty Oh circled the bases. As he crossed the plate, tipped his cap to the crowd, and trotted to the dugout, even the Bears were screaming cheers and jumping up and down.

When they all sat back down, Ahmad turned to the Japanese boy sitting next to him. "Sucker's okay. He can hit, all right. Still think he could use his real name instead of that silly nickname he calls himself."

"That's his real name, Ahmad," Tillyard said. "Oh."

"Since when? You ever see a guy named Oh? Be like Aaron calling himself 'Wow.'"

"Real name Oh," said one of the Japanese boys.

"Okay, okay." Ahmad pursed his lips. "Anyway, sucker can sure hit!"

Tanner and his erstwhile fighting foe got in line at the concession stand, Tanner in front. From somewhere in the rear, the line was pushed, and the boy accidently stepped on Tanner's heel.

Tanner whirled around, shoving the boy with his elbow. The boy stumbled back and bumped into a bunch of sixteen-year-olds, jarring a drink in one of their hands.

The bigger boys were mean-looking, wearing leather jackets with skulls painted on them. They began slapping Tanner's companion around.

Typically not pausing to consider odds or consequences, Tanner reacted like Tanner. He dove at them headfirst, knocking one of them down. He flailed with fists and feet, joined quickly by his friend. The fight became immediately one-sided, the older boys quickly disposing of the younger pair, leaving them seated on the ground, bruised, noses bleeding, clothes torn.

Tanner got up and extended his hand to the other, pulling him erect. He looked over at the concession stand. "Crud. We lost our place in line."

Marvin put on a clean shirt and primped carefully before the mirror, whistling a happy tune.

Rasula watched him grumpily. "Where you goin'?"

"Out."

"What you gonna do?"

"I told you, I have an appointment."

"Anybody can have an appointment."

Marvin looked at him curiously. "That's true, now that I think about it."

"Why didn't you make it a appointment for two, so's I could go?"

Marvin chuckled. "This is an adult appointment, Rasula."

"Adult appointment means just one thing."

Marvin froze. "What?"

"Kids can't go."

He relaxed and laughed. "Right again." He finished combing and primping, said good-bye to Rasula, and left.

Rasula trailed secretly behind.

A few blocks away, Marvin entered a bathhouse.

When he came out an hour later, Rasula was waiting for him in the middle of the sidewalk.

"Well, Rasula," Marvin said, frowning slightly, "fancy meeting you here."

"Not so fancy," Rasula said grimly. "What were you doing in there?"

"Taking a bath."

Rasula scampered along to keep up with him. "There was ladies in there."

"Yup."

"You don't take baths with no ladies."

"In Japan you do. It's the custom."

"I don't know about custom, but I do know about Feldman. You better not let him know about this."

Margin threw an arm around his shoulders and chortled. "Right. It'll be our secret, just you and me."

Rasula grinned happily and leaned against him as they headed back for the hotel.

Kelly and Alika dallied in the park through the evening, then he walked her home. In front of her door, he gave her a hug, somewhat to her discomfort and very much to the disapproval of her father, who peeked out through the curtains.

By the time he got back to the hotel, the Bears had returned from the game, exhausted but still excited with the experience.

"Where you been, Kelly?" Rasula asked.

"Out."

"Gettin' a bath?"

"What?"

Rasula noticed Marvin give a slight shake of his head. "Nothin'."

"What's the matter?" Kelly loked around the room. "Do I stink or something? I took a bath last night."

"Nothing, I said," Rasula said.

133

"Geez, guy could go crazy around here trying to figure out what you talk about, Rasula."

"Lay off Little Bro," Ahmad said firmly.

"Geez." Kelly flopped down on the floor, thinking about Alika.

It was a bright, sunny day. To the Bears, it seemed like it must never rain in Japan—just like Southern California—and it made them feel more at home.

They sat around the suite relaxing, reading newspapers and magazines.

Kelly, humming happily, was combing his hair before going out. Marvin was on the phone.

Tanner scowled at the magazine he was reading, and hurled it to the floor. "Everything you read about the game is how lousy we are and how we shouldn't even be here."

"Well, they're all in for a big surprise," Kelly said, surprising the rest of them with his optimism and spirit. "I'll tell you that."

"Stein's fastball is really starting to happen," Engelberg said. "Really burning them in there. My hand is sore already."

"You're rubbing your right hand, dumbo," Ahmad said. "That ain't the hand you catch with."

"So? Who says I can't rub whichever hand I want?" Stein moved his pitching arm around proudly.

Kelly sidled toward the door, then turned to face the group. "I guarantee I go four-for-four. Bye, guys."

They waved good-byes, pleased with his good humor and the prospects of a hale and happy Kelly Leak at the plate.

"Kelly's really up lately," Toby said. "That's a good sign."

They nodded.

Marvin strolled around, the phone locked to his ear. ". . . Keith Jackson's perfect. Almost as good as Vin Scully. But you got to get somebody like Tom Seaver to do the color. He's the only athlete around who can speak more than four words that make sense. . . . Hold on. . . ."

Rasula was tugging at his pants. "Time to go to the mosque," he whispered.

Marvin cupped his hand over the receiver. "The photographer is taking you two to the mosque. Come on, these trans-Pacific calls cost a fortune."

"But you promised," he whined.

"Okay, okay. I don't know why you two can't just, well, go ahead with the photographer, and just face toward Mecca or something and look like you're praying. Isn't that how it's done?"

"No, Marvin," Ahmad said, sighing, "it's not."

"Well, I don't—okay, let me finish up. Now then"— he returned to the phone—"what do you mean, Seaver comes too high? You think Reggie Jackson or Willy Mays would come any cheaper? . . . Well, just so it's a big name. I gotta run . . . What? . . . To some blamed Moslem mosque. . . . Yeah, thought it would show how we're all together religiously, ethnically, racially. . . . No, it won't backfire. Talk to you later. . . ."

Ahmad, Rasula, Marvin, and a photographer arrived at the mosque and got out of the cab. Marvin maneuvered Rasula in front of the entrance and turned to the photographer. "Let's get one of Rasula alone first."

"What we need more pictures for?" Ahmad asked, a bit annoyed. "Especially here?"

"TV people want as many stills as we can give 'em,

for promotion of the game. Big smile, now, Rasula."

The photographer snapped away.

Ahmad kicked the dirt peevishly.

"Don't worry, Ahmad," Marvin said. "There'll be plenty with you in them."

"That ain't the point."

"Come on," he motioned to the entrance, "let's get a couple shots of both of you inside."

"No."

"What?"

"You don't take no pictures inside a mosque."

"Oh. I didn't know. Okay, glad you told me. I want to show every respect."

"But we still wanna go in, Rasula and me."

"Oh, really? I didn't know you boys were believers."

"Lot of stuff you didn't know, Marvin, and can't never know."

"Unh, okay. We'll wait for you here." He glanced at his watch. "You gonna be long? I mean, does it take long, to do what you do in there?"

"Takes just the right amount of time, Marvin. Come on, Little Bro."

Kelly peered in through the window of the Pachinko parlor. Beyond some of the crowd, he saw Alika arguing with her father. She seemed near tears. Kelly could guess what the subject of the debate was, and it hurt him. In truth, he meant no harm. He wanted to understand the different customs of Japan, but he assumed that affairs of the heart were the same everywhere.

When finally her father left her and went into the back, Kelly caught Alika's attention and waved.

She looked pale, and didn't respond. She returned to her work dispensing the steel balls.

Her father came back to her, saw Kelly at the window, and directed Alika to go outside.

She came obediently out.

He stepped close to her, but she turned away.

Kelly felt awkward. "Well, hi, at least. I'm a little early, hunh? Where you want to eat?"

She shook her head.

"But what about lunch? I thought we had it planned."

"No lunch."

"Oh? Too busy, hunh. Well"—he tried to hide his disappointment—"what about later? How about a movie, after work? Movie, you know?"

"No." She glanced back at the window, where her father was watching. "No more." She struggled with English. "No more see."

"Oh." Kelly shuffled his feet, feeling very uncomfortable and confused and disheartened. "But, well, I'll be going home, tomorrow night, you know. After the game. Back to California. Tomorrow, understand? Can I see you before I go?"

She shook her head violently. "No. Father no like. No more see."

"But, but," Kelly sniffed, "your dad? But why? I didn't do anything to him. Why would he—"

"No same." She slowly reached out to take his hand and held it up beside hers. "No same. Skin no same. See?"

Kelly was stunned. The slight color difference between them had not occurred to him. "Geez, people are like that—even here? I thought we had a lock on that kind of stuff in the United States. Gosh, I—"

"No more see." She turned abruptly and went back inside.

Kelly watched through the window. She returned to her work, but he could see tears on her cheeks.

He jammed his hands in his pockets and walked away.

He walked sadly through the Tokyo streets, wrestling with the swells of rage and frustration that welled up in him. He passed the familiar row of motorcycles where he had stopped once before. He heard the cackling laughter of the bikers inside the cafe.

He squared his shoulders, looked down the row of bikes, then strode purposefully toward the one he had admired before.

It was a beauty, all right—a chopped and chromed, four-cylinder, 1,000-cc Yamaha.

He straddled it, kicked down on the starter, and listened to the engine roar to life. He revved it several times, looking at the cafe.

Then, when the first biker appeared at the door, he took off, spinning the rear wheel on the pavement.

Whizzing down the street, zigzagging among the cars, he glanced behind him to see several bikers roaring in pursuit. He took a sharp right turn, then a left. They were gaining on him.

Near the hotel, he skidded to a stop, got off, pointed the front end of the bike toward a brick building, popped the clutch, and watched the Yamaha go slamming wildly into the wall.

He dashed off, losing himself in the crowd of people and cars just as the bikers arrived at the scene.

Marvin returned to the hotel, the two brothers in tow, and went to the front desk for messages. There were none. He stood looking wistfully at the empty pigeonhole above his room number where messages would be left. He stood looking at it as if at any moment a message would appear there.

From behind, a well-dressed, tightly muscled man of about thirty, wearing dark sunglasses, approached and tapped him on the shoulder.

Marvin spun around as if zapped by a cattle prod. "Louie!" His face broke into a grin. "What in blazes are you doing here?"

Louie hugged him happily. "Wouldn't miss your big moment for the world, fella."

"Buddy old buddy," Marvin said, clapping him on the back.

"Marvin, old friend."

Marvin pushed away and looked at him. "Okay, really now, what's up?"

"Here with some friends, on business."

"Business? In Japan?"

"No place is hotter, business-wise, than the old land of the rising sun, old chum."

"I guess you're right."

"So anyway"—Louie took his arm and steered him toward the door—"I promised my friends I'd introduce you to them."

Marvin hesitated. "Unh, Louie, you're not upset, are you, you know, about what I owe you?"

"Hey." Louie held up his palms. "What's an old debt among friends?"

"Sometimes it's a problem, Louie," Marvin said carefully.

"Hey, no. Come on now." He pushed open the door. "This trip is just friendly business. And you're my friend. And you just might be interested in my business."

"Your business is always fascinating, Louie, even if it does bring certain ethical questions into play."

"You know what I always say about that. . . ."

"Yeah. Ethical shmethical."

They went out, laughing.

In Louie's fine, well-furnished suite at the Hilton—a Western-style environment Marvin envied—Marvin was introduced to two other young men with drinks in their hands. They welcomed him warmly and pleasantly, and he took a seat.

"Yessirree, we been following your activities over here all we could," said one of them, with a smooth southern accent. "And that wrestling match—didn't that beat all? We heard about it, but sure wish we coulda seen it. I tell you, it sounded just about the wackiest thing I ever heard."

"Well, everything you heard," Marvin said, "you can multiply by three. Because it was insane." Louie's two companions roared with laughter and slapped their thighs. "I mean, we could get psychiatric testimony to that fact. Those boys just went plumb out of their skulls. And the wrestler!" They roared expectantly. "He was dancing around like he was stepping on cactuses, my boys hanging off him every which way, biting and scratching and poking. It's something I wouldn't want to try again, I'll tell you that!"

When their hilarity had subsided, Louie said, "So when Marvin here calls me and says he wants me to get a line on a kids' baseball game, I think: all right, this is it. Marvin's always been on the edge, and now he's finally gone." He nodded at them while they laughed some more. "But I lay it down on the betting boards anyway, just as a joke. Inside five days people just couldn't stay away from it. Heck, it was part patriotism, part paternal, part who-knows-what-all."

"Well, you know it is," said the southerner. "Somebody's laying book, some people'll bet on anything."

"And this was something brand-new," said the other man. "Everybody wants to get in on a thing first time around."

"Nobody understands that better than my old friend Louie," Marvin said, looking proudly at him. "What are the odds now, Louie?"

"Twenty-five to one, last time I hung up the phone. And money is still pouring in on the Japanese team."

"Some patriotism," the man said.

"Tellin' you though," said the southerner, "what you and those boys have done, comin' over here, takin' up that challenge—really something. I mean really. Folks where I come from admire a man with that kinda moxie. Know what I mean? Give 'em a two-fisted risk-taker every time."

Marvin nodded. "It's been some experience, I'll say."

"Only bum thing about it is," the southerner went on, "those boys have endeared themselves to a good handful of folks back home, and it's just a cryin' shame they don't have a better chance. Heck, folks don't want to see them comin' all the way over here just to *lose*."

"Well, I'll tell you," Marvin said thoughtfully, "that Japanese team is super. I mean it. I mean, at every single position they've got an all-star. Quick gloves, quick bats, quick feet on the basepaths—"

"And it's a cryin' shame things can't be evened out a little bit."

Marvin looked at him. "It's a little late for that. We can't turn our stumblebums into all-stars over night, no matter how hard we—or they—try."

"Nope. That's a fact." The southerner watched Marvin drain his drink. "But we weren't really suggesting that, Mr. Lazar."

The sudden formal address alerted Marvin. Something was up, all right.

Louie got up and opened a door to the next room. "Boys?" he called inside.

Three "boys" came shyly into the room. All were nearly six feet tall, and one seemed taller.

"Marvin," Louie said, gesturing grandly toward the three, "like you to meet Henry, Mitch, and Jethro." The boys shifted their feet uncomfortably as Marvin nodded greetings. "Why don't you boys go on downstairs and get yourself a snack, hunh?"

They nodded and walked out.

Marvin watched them leave, his eyes hardened cynically.

"The big one, Henry," the southerner grinned, "got a fastball what snaps off like a limb fallin' off a tree."

"When does he turn thirty?" Marvin asked softly.

"No, no," said the other man, waving his hand, "they're all the right age, give or take."

"Just tall," the southerner said. "And as a matter of fact, they're all from California—same as your boys. That makes it all Jim Dandy."

"Yeah." Marvin was amused. "With the possible exception that they aren't exactly members of our team."

"Sure they are. Now."

"Okay," Marvin sighed, "what is it, gentlemen?"

"Well now." The southerner paced back and forth. "To begin with, you got no set roster. Not officially, that is. I mean, your team list ain't got no notary-public seal on it. And you only got ten youngsters. That's a light list by any standard. Shoot, nobody expects you to go out there without a bench of reserves. Supposing somebody got hurt, or sick?"

"Supposing."

142

"You got to have a bunch of reserves to run in there. Unh, freshen up your glass a mite?"

"No thanks."

The room was silent for a few moments.

The southerner turned toward Marvin, smiling with one side of his mouth. "We could sure make things worth your while, Marvin."

"Yeah." He shot a glare at Louie. "I'll bet you could."

"Look now, old buddy," Louie said, gripping the back of Marvin's neck tenderly, "I generated a lot of interest in Nevada on this thing for you—just like you asked me to do, as a favor. I don't want to say you owe me, but it's not the first time I've been there when you needed something."

"Old debts, hunh?"

"Hey—"

"Sorry, didn't mean that. You've always been a prince, Louie, a prince. I'm grateful."

"Just how grateful?"

Marvin looked around the room. He leaned back against the headrest of the chair and folded his hands behind his neck. "Grateful enough."

"Well, that's fine, then," the southerner drawled, nodding around. "We got a program."

Kelly lay on his quilt, staring moodily at the ceiling.

Engelberg nodded at him. "Well, guys, he's back to his old self again."

"Yeah," Ahmad said. "Makes me feel right at home."

"I think perhaps Kelly is ready," Feldman intoned, "for a refresher course with the Lord."

"Cool it." Kelly's soft voice carried enough menace to shut them up.

Marvin threw open the door and strode in, hyperactive with energy, flashing a mechanical smile. "Well, boys, old Marvin's come through again. Yes sir. When you're starvin', depend on Marvin."

Ahmad chuckled wryly. "Either you jazzin' or you razzin'."

"Neither. I'm granting you your original wish."

The boys gathered around.

"What was that?" Engelberg asked.

Marvin flung the door open wider and swept his arm around, beckoning inward. The three new boys came into the room, looking a little sheepish.

"Here are your ringers, boys," Marvin said. "Henry, pitcher. Mitch, center field. Jethro, first base."

The Bears stood gaping at the newcomers.

"You guys were so worried about losing," Marvin said, "I decided to do something about it." He firmed his voice. "Darned if I'm gonna let you guys get embarrassed out there tomorrow!"

After an awkward pause, during which the Bears looked at each other, Toby spoke up. "Marvin, do you mind if we talk with you alone?"

"No, of course not. Henry, could you three wait in the next room a minute?"

They went quickly out.

"So?" Marvin looked around the bunch of Bears. "What is it?"

"Well—"

"You see—"

"Maybe I'm just speaking for myself," Toby said, "but I don't think we need any help, not this kind of help."

"Hunh?"

"Darn right we don't," Tanner said, pushing out his jaw.

They all nodded.

"What's this all of a sudden?" Marvin held out his hands.

"We can handle it by ourselves," Ahmad said.

Marvin narrowed his eyes. "That wasn't your tune when we first met."

"You wasn't exactly playin' *us* the same tune neither, Marvin," Ahmad said.

"And things have changed," Tillyard said, straightening his glasses on his nose.

"You pushed that underdog thing so hard," Tanner piped up, "that now everybody thinks we're just a bunch of spaz cruds. And we got something to prove."

"And you'll prove it tomorrow." Marvin began to get irritated. "And those kids can help. I didn't get a whole regiment, after all."

"It's not right," Feldman said.

Marvin slapped his hands down on his hips. His voice rose. "So that's it. I think I'm doing you a favor —saving you from humiliation—and I just get slapped in the face for it." He blinked rapidly. "I mean, you've seen that Japanese team. They are the New York Yankees, for Pete's sake!"

"You didn't care about that a few days ago," Tillyard said.

Exasperated, Marvin slumped into a chair. The Bears stood looking at him. "All right, let me tell you why these ringers are important. If it's a close game or we win, you're like heroes. When you get back home, there's more promos, commercials, exhibitions, endorsements—whatever. It means more money for you —not just a little more, tons! But if you get slaughtered out there, humiliated, ground into the dirt, then it's all over. This whole things ends up on the junk pile."

145

"Let *us* worry about that," Engelberg said.

Marvin scanned the group, shaking his head. "You know our contract says I can do anything I want along these lines."

They stared back at him silently. For a time he looked at the floor. Then he sighed and straightened up. "But to heck with it. I'm not going to hold you to it. We've been through too much for me to start getting ugly. I'm too professional for that." He nodded coldly to them. "If you boys don't think I'm doing the best thing for all of us, just tell me, and I'll tear up those contracts and toss 'em out the window."

The Bears looked at each other, more nervously now.

"I don't get it," Toby said. "What happens then?"

"Yeah, what happens to the game?" Tanner asked in a quavering voice.

"The game's fine," Marvin said calmly. "You go out there, you play." He sighed wearily. "I'll get someone good to negotiate a new deal for you."

"What kinda someone?" Ahmad asked.

"That's my worry. Someone good."

There was a pause.

"But what do you get, Marvin?" Tillyard asked.

"What I get I already got."

The boys began to look guilty, all except for Ahmad, who eyed Marvin with growing anger.

"Look," Marvin went on, "you guys make the decision. And I see some guilty faces. Don't feel guilty. You don't owe me a darned thing. If it wasn't for you, none of us would be here. If anything, I owe *you*."

The boys stammered at each other, hemming and hawing, shuffling their feet.

"Well," Stein said softly, at last, "I guess I don't really have to pitch."

"And I don't have to play first base," Toby said, even more softly, "long as we win—that's the most important thing. I guess."

"Okay." Marvin waved toward the next room. "Then we got a program. Why don't you guys go and greet your new teammates? Go get to know each other. Go get a Coke or something. Take whatever you need out of my wallet." He smiled warmly.

But the boys didn't smile back, nor did they take any money. Spiritlessly, they drifted into the next room to make introductions to the three ringers.

Marvin got up wearily and ambled over to the dresser. He yawned and poured a drink.

"That was some of your best crap you threw there, Marvin."

"What?" Marvin spun around to see Ahmad still in the room.

"You like to save the best for last, hmm?" Ahmad's eyes sparkled with anger. "And they really bought it too. All of 'em. 'Cept for me."

"Unh, what are you driving at, Ahmad?"

"What's your deal? What you got going with those ringers?"

"Nothing," Marvin said quickly, too quickly.

"Unh-hunh. Gonna tear up our contracts, hunh? Mister Big Heart. Going to help us out, let us free. And let yourself free too, coincidentally."

"I don't know what you're driving at. I was serious when I made that offer."

"Yeah, I know." He paused. "Oh, you were serious, all right. Serious as a heart attack. But you ain't about to let us out of nothin'!"

Marvin sipped his drink uneasily. Ahmad's eyes burned into him.

"You buzz our behinds over here, hustle us around,

147

cheatin' and lyin' every place you go. And then you go make out like we owe you the world!"

"I told you, you owe me nothing. Like I said, if anything, I owe—"

"I ain't no chump, mister! If I'm dyin', I ain't buyin'!"

"What do you have to buy? You can see the truth for yourself. I got us the game, didn't I? You had no game without me."

"You got us a freak show! We came here to play a ball game!"

"Well, I'm sorry you feel that way, Ahmad."

"Don't give me that soft talk," Ahmad snorted. "And dragging my brother all over the place like he's some puppy dog, talkin' 'bout his fine kisser and how people love him and all that."

"I like Rasula. So do a lot of people."

"What you like is a cute little black boy with a big smile who don't mind you stickin' a camera in his face every time he turns around."

Marvin winced. "That's a very harsh thing to say. It hurts me that you even think that."

"More jive! You ain't hurt. You ain't never been hurt. Only real live people get hurt." He headed for the door, then stopped and turned. "You said you been down for fifteen years. You ever stop to think why?"

"It's a tough business I'm in."

"Maybe, maybe not. But that ain't it. If you got to be some real big shot, you'd still be down. You were made to be down."

He slammed the door behind him.

EIGHT

Game day dawned with a queer feeling to it, for Marvin. Except for him, the suite was empty.

He dressed quickly and went down to join the Bears for breakfast.

There were very few people in the hotel coffee shop, and no Bears. The three new additions to the team—the ringers—sat at a large table.

Marvin pulled out a chair beside them. "Where's the crew?"

The big boys shrugged. "Haven't seen 'em," said Jethro.

"Not at all?"

"Nope."

"Must've eaten in a hurry."

"We been here an hour, Mr. Lazer. Ever since the place opened for breakfast."

"Must be giving the town one more swing."

"That's probably it, Mr. Lazar."

"They shouldn't have skipped breakfast, though."

"Nope."

Marvin kept looking around, half expecting the team to come through the door at any moment. "Well, I'll catch up with them somewhere. Tell me something, are you guys really good?"

"Depends on who you compare us to, Mr. Lazar," Henry said. "Compared to the Yankees, we're not so hot. Compared to your team, we're, well—"

"Hot?"

"I guess that's about it—not to brag about it."

Marvin sighed. "Hope it's worth it," he mumbled. Then more loudly, "You guys ready to play?"

"Don't think I'm being sassy," Mitch said, "but that's what we came for. Isn't that right?"

"Right, right. Listen, you guys go ahead and eat. Think I'll mosey around a little, catch up with the tykes, make sure they get their nourishment. They probably feel too excited to eat, but they need their strength."

"Yes, sir. Thank you."

The Japanese team, in casual clothes, was already wolfing down Big Macs and Egg McMuffins when the Bears joined them at McDonald's. As usual among them, little was said, much was understood. There were many smiles and nods.

The host team finished, then waited for the Bears to get through. They all left together.

They went on a kind of tour. But not downtown. They wandered to the outskirts, a residential section, where they ambled along the pleasant streets looking at what were, to the Bears, extremely neat and quite fragile and entirely interesting homes. Nothing needed to be explained or pointed out to them. They saw everything, and imagined more. Among themselves, the Bears chatted about the scenes, exchanging impressions and perceptions.

The Bears didn't know much at all about Japan. They didn't need to be told that—not now. They knew they knew even less now, in important ways, than they thought they knew when they had arrived.

But one thing they knew for sure, and they hadn't known that when they came: Regardless of baseball talent, the Bears and the Far Eastern Champs were in the same league—in the ways that mattered.

They had lots of time to kill before afternoon, when they would play baseball against each other.

At noon, Alika left the Pachinko parlor. She was glum, but walked quickly.

It was a good while, and some distance, before she reached the hotel. The clerk smiled at seeing her familiar face, and greeted her warmly.

"But," he told her, "I'm afraid your young friend is not here."

"I know," she said softly. "I would just like to leave him a note—a sort of good-bye—if you would be so kind as to take it for me."

"It would be an honor," he said, bowing.

She printed the note very carefully, her tongue between her lips. The clerk handed her an envelope. She put the note in it, sealed it, and handed it back. She watched to be sure the clerk put it in the proper pigeonhole.

"I am grateful for your attention," she said, bowing.

"I am honored to be of service," he said, bowing back. "But you should be of better cheer, young lady." He smiled. "Today is the day of the big game."

"I know. Thank you."

She left, miserable.

Marvin searched everywhere he could think of, for as long as he could, before going to the stadium.

Early fans were already beginning to fill the seats. Clearly the crowd would fulfill his expectations.

Walking onto the field, he was surprised to see, across the way, that the Japanese team was not in its dugout. Coach Shimizu was berating an assistant, who shook his head and held up his hands.

Marvin beckoned to the translator, and walked over.

Before he could say anything, Shimizu confronted him frantically. "Not here! Nobody! Not mine, not yours! TV people going crazy!"

In the Bears' dugout were only the three new boys wearing the new Bears uniforms, and a very nervous program director.

Marvin approached the dugout tentatively, trying to figure out what he should say, and beyond that what the truth was. He decided to tell the agitated program director the truth as far as he knew it.

"I can't find them," he said.

"What? What do you mean?" The director waved his arms as if swatting flies.

"I looked all over. Nobody's seen them this morning."

"Holy moley! You know what this means?"

"It means they're a little late."

"A little late. A little late! You pulling some kind of number, Lazar? We go on the air with the pregame in twenty minutes! Looka the crowd!"

"Yeah, I see. Terrific crowd. Just like I promised."

"Yeah! But who's gonna play in the darned *game?*"

"They'll be here. They're just boys, don't watch the clock as closely as we do. I already got three players here, as you can see."

"Yeah. I never seen them before. Where you been keeping 'em?"

"Under wraps. I'll go make a couple phone calls."

"You do that, Lazar! And make one to your lawyer, if you don't find your team!"

In the press box, Marvin ran into Shimizu, who was rapidly trying to explain the situation to some executive types in pinstripe suits. It was clear by their expressions that these executives were not at all pleased with what they were hearing.

Marvin reached for the phone, then realized he had nobody to call. He sat down on a stool, rested his chin in his hands, and stared down at the empty playing field.

It took some time for the boys to cut out the cardboard just right and get it set firmly into the dirt. But when done, it looked like a pretty decent home plate.

The two teams nodded approval and went to their positions—the Japanese taking the field and the Bears sitting on the grass to one side, waiting their turns at bat.

No crowd saw this action, for it took place in the grubby little park behind the hotel—the only place the two teams figured they could play a decent game of baseball without being bothered and interfered with by agents, promoters, TV types, coaches, and other meddling adults.

This was, they had all agreed without having to say it, what they had come to do.

Ahmad stepped up as the lead-off batter, and tapped the cardboard plate with his bat.

In time, having no place else to go, Marvin returned to the dugout, now hopeless and grouchy. The three boys and Louie's two gamblers were there.

"Somethin' darned fishy about all this," the southerner said. "Now, you wouldn't be knowin' a thing or two about this that you ain't tellin', hunh, Marvin?"

"Nope." Marvin felt like breaking his neck—or somebody's. "All I know is what you see."

"Which is no team."

"Right."

The man narrowed his eyes meanly, and spoke in an understated way that carried an implied threat. "We come a long way, Marvin."

"That's right. You guys traveled pretty far to see this ball game. And I don't like to see you disappointed. So why don't you young hotshots go on out there." He handed the ringers a ball. "Toss this around a while and give these gents a show."

Louie arrived to hear the last. "Don't get flip, Marvin."

"Who, me?"

"This is serious."

Marvin's anger rose. "You bet it is, serious as a heart attack. I'm responsible for putting on a baseball game here."

"That's right."

"And it hasn't been canceled yet, not officially."

"That's right."

"So it just occurred to me that this is still my Bears' dugout."

"So?"

"So it further occurred to me that you're in my dugout. Move out."

"What?"

"Beat it. And take your three ringers with you."

"Hold it, bud, you can't—"

"Unless you want me to call a cop." Marvin pointed out to the group of security guards standing near the seats.

154

Scowling and red-faced, Louie and his cohorts backed out of the dugout and stomped away.

When Alika left the hotel, she decided to go the long way back. That took her near the park. She heard American voices and turned toward them. She saw them playing, saw Kelly at bat. She smiled gloriously and ran over.

Kelly took a vicious swing, and missed. He was not concentrating. His thoughts were elsewhere. Then he heard her cheering voice, and saw her running into the park, her gorgeous hair bouncing on her shoulders.

He felt a surge of strength and stepped back up to the plate. The next pitch was grooved, and Kelly laced it deep over the center-fielder's head. He tore around the bases and, crossing home plate, dove into Alika's arms.

The Bears mobbed them, and all together they danced around in a clump, waving fists and cheering.

According to Tillyard, who kept such statistics in his head, they had just tied the game.

Marvin sat disconsolately in the dugout, his mood not improved by the bitter ranting of the program director.

"This could cost me my job, Lazar."

"I know. Sorry. Mine too. But it's not over until they say it's over, officially."

At which instant, the public-address system crackled with an announcement. The large crowd groaned. Then thousands of boos filled the air. Spectators waved fists and threw programs and seat cushions down onto the field.

"It's official," Marvin said, leaning his chin in his hands.

The director closed his eyes and leaned his forehead against the dugout wall. Slowly he turned back around. "Lot of raincheck money to pay out."

"I had twenty-five percent of the gate," Marvin said absently.

"My whole career in the balance," the director moaned. He brightened a bit. "Listen, Lazar, you still think there's a chance they'll show?"

"Sure."

"Okay. Long as there's a chance. We'll leave the cameras in place and tape it without the crowd, when your boys get here."

"Good idea," Marvin said without feeling.

"But at four o'clock we lose the sunlight. So if you and the new Japanese coach can find your teams by four, let us know."

Marvin looked up, startled, as if just freshly awakened. "New Japanese coach?"

"Yeah, the other one resigned or got fired. Big disgrace. Lose face, as they say. The federation his team belonged to just didn't take this lightly. I sure wish we had federations of our own to deal with people like you."

"Good idea."

Marvin left and headed for the other dugout, where Shimizu sat with his head buried in his hands. Sitting down beside him, Marvin put an arm around his shoulders. "Sorry, old buddy."

Shimizu looked up, muttered something, shrugged, and shook his head.

"What do you say you and me get the heck out of here and go back to my suite, and . . ." He pantomimed taking a drink.

Shimizu smiled. "You got Johnny Walker Black Label?"

* * *

Bearing down hard, Stein fired a fastball past the strong Japanese hitter for strike three.

The Bears at their positions erupted in cheers. After getting the bases loaded, the Far Eastern Champs hadn't scored. Stein had the groove.

For some reason, the Bears were hanging in. By Tillyard's reckoning, the Bears were scoring every time the Japanese were—more or less. In any case, it was a tight and intensely played game. It was the very model of a fine game of baseball played by young teams. Any coach or parent would have been proud of them.

Jimmy Feldman beat out a grounder to deep third. On the first pitch to Tanner, Feldman tried to steal second. He slid, the shortstop slapped on the tag.

It was a close play. The shortstop said he was out. But the second-baseman said he was safe. The two Japanese players argued as if on opposing teams.

There being no umpire to settle the dispute, Feldman himself settled it. He looked skyward for a moment, sighed, and walked off the field.

"Hey, you were safe!" Tanner yelled.

"I thought so too," Feldman said.

"Then what in blazes are you doing?"

Feldman pointed at the sky. "I could just tell that He didn't think I was safe."

"Get a pair of glasses!" Tanner yelled at the sky.

The two men were awash in pain and suffering. Marvin paced, mumbling and sipping his drink. Shimizu groaned loudly, sipping his.

"Well, don't lose your cool, Shimizu. Worst comes to worst, I'll get you a job in West Hollywood. Ever do any gardening?"

157

Shimizu shook his head and dismissed the idea with a wave of his hand.

"Job market's tough in Hollywood now, though," Marvin went on. "You should've been there in the forties. You would have made a fortune in war movies. One picture after another. Of course you would've played in mainly death scenes. You know, John Wayne blasting you out of trees and kicking your teeth in."

Shimizu covered his mouth protectively. Then he let out a scream.

Marvin whirled toward him, expecting to see the worst.

But Shimizu had not committed suicide. He was standing at the window, pointing down, his mouth hanging open, his eyes wide as balloons.

Marvin looked out, seeing nothing unusual at first. Then, "Great Scott! It's *them!* I don't believe it!" Frantically he pulled at his sleeve, trying to find his watch. "What time is it? We must have enough time! Loads of time!" He grabbed the phone and hollered into it, "Get me Yomiuri Stadium, hurry, it's an emer—"

But then he looked at Shimizu and slowly hung up the receiver. "Yeah, I know what you mean. Let's just forget all that."

Shimizu nodded agreement.

"Let's go watch the game."

They trotted down the hallway and down the stairs and out to the park.

By the time they arrived, the game had just ended. The boys from both teams were sitting around, tired and fulfilled, chatting as best they could with what little language they shared. Kelly and Alika sat leaning against each other.

Marvin and Shimizu sat down in the dirt with them.

158

All at once a small crowd came running into the park. It was the ABC program director, the gamblers, and several reporters.

"What in the world are you all doing here!" screeched the director breathlessly, holding his chest as he stumbled to a stop.

"Don't feel bad," Marvin said. "We missed it too. How'd you find out about it?"

"We were followin' you, Marvin," the southerner said, showing his mean smile. "Figured you were trying to pull something tricky."

"Lazar! Step on it!" the director cried, pushing the other men away. "Get their uniforms on them and get over to the stadium! We can still shoot a few minutes!"

"They've already played," Marvin said listlessly.

"What? Our contract with you says you got to deliver us a game!"

"I delivered it, in a way. They played it here instead of there, is all. And the contract doesn't say anything about a double-header."

Gurgling noises came from the director's throat.

The southerner stepped up to the boys. "Unh, who won, fellas?"

"It was a close game," Tanner said.

"But who won? It's important. We had a lot of chips riding on it."

"We don't know, for sure," Engelberg said, putting a finger beside his cheek.

"I lost track," Tillyard said.

"It was close, though," Tanner said.

"Lazar, I'm going to see that the network sues you black and blue," the director rasped.

Marvin shrugged. "So sue." He opened his wallet. "Here's my Sears charge card. Take it, use it toward the settlement. I'm no longer promoting, producing, hyping. You want them to play? Then you ask them yourself. I'm out of the business. Right, Ahmad?"

"You're getting there," he said smiling.

"I think it's happened," Feldman said, looking skyward, his face a rosy glow.

"Now why don't all you men just get yourself on out of here," Marvin said, "and let Coach Shimizu and me have these last few minutes together in peace."

The director, gamblers, and reporters left, showing varying degrees of resentment, rage, and disappointment.

The Bears and the Far Eastern Champions gathered in a circle, sitting on the dirt to exchange words and hand signals about the game.

Marvin took Shimizu's elbow and led him off a ways. He leaned close to the coach's ear and whispered, "Cuba."

"What?"

"We'll take both teams. Play a round-robin with the Cuban champs. We'll make a million, believe me, listen to old Marvin. . . ."